PUFFIN BOOKS

GOLDEN PENNIES

It is in a mood of hope and expectation that the Greenwood family set off to seek their fortune in the goldfields of Ballarat, in southern Australia, in 1851. The city life they are leaving behind them seems to have nothing but poverty and hardship to offer. For fourteen-year-old Jack the excitement and promise of a new life is marred only by his dislike and resentfulness of his stepfather Luke.

However, the family's hopes are dashed before they even reach their destination: their coach is ambushed and bushrangers make off with almost all they possess. When they *do* reach Jericho – a dismal, harsh shanty-town – the hostility and apathy they meet merely add to their disappointment and despair.

The family's grim struggle for survival in the goldfields, the back-breaking work, the friends and enemies they make and the dangerous adventure they find themselves involved in make exciting reading. This is a gripping story, peopled by a fascinating variety of characters, based on the successful television series.

Graeme Farmer

GOLDEN
PENNIES

PUFFIN BOOKS

Puffin Books, Penguin Books Ltd, Harmondsworth, Middlesex, England
Viking Penguin Inc., 40 West 23rd Street, New York, New York 10010, U.S.A.
Penguin Books Australia Ltd, Ringwood, Victoria, Australia
Penguin Books Canada Ltd, 2801 John Street, Markham, Ontario, Canada L3R 1B4
Penguin Books (N.Z.) Ltd, 182–190 Wairau Road, Auckland 10, New Zealand

First published 1985

Made and printed in Great Britain by
Richard Clay (The Chaucer Press) Ltd,
Bungay, Suffolk
Filmset in 10 on 13 Photina by
Northumberland Press Ltd, Gateshead,
Tyne and Wear

CHAPTER ONE

Jack felt slightly sick from the continual jolting and swaying of the coach; but so absorbed was he in the surroundings, he took no notice. The countryside through which the rutted, muddy track meandered was heavily clothed in eucalyptus trees and dense undergrowth. It was deep green and glossy from the winter rains. Jack had lived in a town all his fourteen years so had never seen bush as thick and forbidding.

The coach was approaching another couple of diggers trudging wearily along the verge of the slippery track. They had passed hundreds of such men, and some women and children as well, who had set out from Melbourne for the goldfields hoping to make their fortunes. The lure of riches must have been very strong – so many of them looked more dead than alive, gaunt from the struggle of travel and hunger, bedraggled from the mud and the rain, and haunted from the unending and empty bush. Jack caught his sister's eye. A frown gathered on Lucy's pretty face. She was even more upset by their wretched condition, perhaps because she was only twelve.

Rebecca, their mother, put her hand on Lucy's to comfort her. She smiled at Jack. No matter how badly Jack felt, a smile from his beautiful mother improved his mood. He looked around to find his stepfather Luke smiling at his mother and sister. Even though his real father had been dead for over two years, and Luke and Rebecca married for half that time, Jack still resented seeing the three of them getting on so well.

Jack caught sight of a group of kangaroos grazing in a small valley which fell away to one side. He grinned. They looked so odd with their tiny shoulders and arms, and their powerful legs and huge tail. They snuffed the air and bounded off into the foliage.

'Are you all right, Jack?' Luke asked.

'Yes,' Jack replied curtly.

Luke looked hurt, as he always did when Jack rebuffed him.

'How much longer will it be?' Lucy asked.

'It can't be much longer,' Rebecca said.

'No, I'm sure it can't,' Luke agreed.

'You've been saying that for the past three hours,' Jack complained.

Rebecca shot Jack a reproving look. 'Don't be cheeky!' she said.

Luke turned to the only other passenger. 'How far is it to Jericho?'

The silent and morose government clerk slowly lowered his book and fixed Luke with a hard stare, then turned it on the rest of the family. 'Miles away yet, as it should be.'

Nobody was quite sure what he meant, and Luke frowned questioningly.

'The goldfields are places of lawlessness, dirt and evil, so it is fitting that they should be miles away from civilization.'

The Greenwoods shifted uncomfortably under his gaze.

The humourless man seemed to warm to his theme. 'And

Jericho is worse than most. More fool them who go there of their own accord.'

Luke didn't wish to pursue the matter in the face of such frostiness.

Suddenly the coach pitched violently and shuddered to a halt. The driver could be heard cursing and urging the horses on. The coach made a number of forward movements before jolting back and staying put.

The driver jumped down and opened the door. 'Ladies and gentlemen, you'll have to step out, I'm afraid. We're stuck in a hole.'

The clerk started to grumble about the inconvenience, but the Greenwoods disembarked as quickly as their creaking limbs would allow.

The coach had become mired in a dip in the track gouged out by stormwater. The driver bit a big piece of tobacco from a quid which he kept in his shirt pocket and chewed on it with determination.

'This shouldn't take too long, folks. Just make yourselves at home.' He then went to the horses' heads and, slipping and sliding, tried to lead them out.

The Greenwoods gazed at their surroundings. The bush seemed to stare resentfully back at the intruders and the sky, heavy with rain, glowered greyly down on them. The one cheerful thing was the clear, liquid call of the bellbird. If water could sing it would sound like that, Lucy thought.

'Could you two gents put your shoulders to the wheel, please,' the driver called.

'This is insufferable,' the clerk griped.

'We won't be shifting from here unless you do,' the driver

advised equably. The clerk and Luke moved to the back of the coach and positioned themselves to push.

'I've paid my fare and expect the horses to pull me to Jericho, not the other way round.'

The coach inched up the incline then slipped back. Luke was splattered with mud. He looked over to his family for sympathy. Rebecca and Lucy smiled but Jack looked back stonily.

So preoccupied were they that they did not notice two masked men appear quietly.

'Bail up! Bail up! Stay right where you are or we'll blow your brains out!' The sudden vicious command startled the travellers out of their wits. One of the bandits, a big hulking brute, had a pistol trained on the men and the other one, skinny and gangling, had a rifle pointed at Rebecca and Jack. They both had kerchiefs tied around the lower part of their faces. They kneed their horses forward without haste, realizing they had everything under control.

Rebecca moved protectively in front of her children.

'You move round here where we can see you!' the big bushranger barked.

Luke rushed to his family's side.

'Now put your hands where I can see them!'

The clerk thrust his hands above his head. The driver's eyes flicked up to where his shotgun was.

The big bushranger noticed this. 'I wouldn't try it.' He rode over, picked the shotgun up and put it in a saddle-holster.

'We're not carrying any gold. You're wasting your time.' The driver disgustedly spat a jet of tobacco juice on the hooves of their horses.

'You might not be, but what about these fine people. Now

listen carefully. If you get it wrong, it might be the last mistake you make.' He grinned with mock-pleasantness. 'My friend will pass amongst you and collect your wallets and purses and jewellery. Don't try to hide anything – we're going to search you. Get on with it, Bones!'

'Right, Ernest.' Ernest was clearly the leader. Bones immediately dismounted and confronted the passengers. The clerk divested himself of his wallet and watch, grinning ingratiatingly.

'That's what I like to see,' Ernest chuckled.

Bones moved on to the Greenwoods. 'Come on, hand it over. All of it.'

'I beg you to think of my wife and children. We're trying to make a new life for ourselves,' Luke pleaded.

'You're breaking my heart,' mocked Ernest.

Bones wrenched a small shoulder reticule from Rebecca and opened it up. 'Now drop your valuables in here. Rings and all.'

Luke dropped his gold watch and ring in.

'And you too, ladies.'

With great reluctance, Rebecca pulled off her wedding ring and a brooch from her lapel. She dropped them into the bag. Luke surreptitiously touched a small bulge under his arm as if to assure himself it was still there.

Ernest's flickering eyes missed nothing. 'What are you hiding?'

'Me? Nothing.' Luke tried to sound convincing.

'What's that under your arm?'

Luke's face fell. His look of horror said it all. 'What? Nothing.' Unfortunately Luke was a bad liar.

Ernest clicked the hammer back on his pistol and stuck it

under Luke's nose. With an apologetic look at his wife, Luke reached into a secret pocket and handed over a chamois pouch.

Although the bottom half of his face was covered, Ernest was obviously licking his lips with greed.

'Please! Please! We'll starve,' Rebecca cried.

Ernest ignored her as he inspected the contents of the pouch. 'Gold pieces *and* a wallet,' he gloated. 'I'm very glad our paths crossed today.'

Jack looked at Lucy. They both knew that the pouch contained all the money they had in the world. They remembered how Rebecca had embroidered Luke's initials on to the supple leather before they left Melbourne and had then sewn a secret pocket into Luke's jacket.

Bones noticed a locket around Lucy's neck and made a grab for it.

'I wouldn't touch her, Mister, she's got the fever,' Jack said.

'Eh?' Bones recoiled.

'Big spots all over her. The Doc said anybody touching her is bound to die.' Lucy provided a dire-sounding cough to back up Jack's story. Bones was clearly one-part bandit and nine-parts coward. He retreated apprehensively.

'Now we're going to search you. You've got one last chance,' Ernest warned.

Jack looked at the bag dangling from Bones' skinny hand. Perhaps it was because Jack had been born with a lame leg that he was always trying to prove he was as brave as everybody else; perhaps it was because Luke had done nothing to prevent the robbers from stealing all their belongings ... Whatever the reason, he decided to do something.

Like an arrow from a bow, Jack launched himself at the bag. He grabbed it and hared off.

Rebecca was the first to realize what was happening. 'Jack ... No! Jack ... No!' she called after him.

Bones gawked stupidly at his empty hand, but Ernest was quick to recover. 'Shoot them if they move,' he snapped over his shoulder as he spurred his horse.

Lucy watched in horror as Ernest closed the gap on her brother. Rebecca was whimpering with anguish and Luke had to hold her back.

Jack ran as fast as he was able over the uneven ground, the bag clutched firmly in his hand. He glanced back at the horseman coming up fast. Ernest could not draw a bead on Jack, because of the pitching of his horse. Jack's leg was beginning to pain him as it always did when he ran fast. He didn't know what to do. He knew he couldn't outdistance the horseman. He ran on blindly, his breath coming in gasps.

Without warning, the ground opened up beneath his feet and he crashed head-first into a shallow mine-shaft. Everything went black for a moment. He heard the horse's hooves approach and stop. He was glad it was breathing so hard because this covered his own panting. He stared up through the dense undergrowth which had broken his fall.

Ernest scanned the bush in perplexity. He couldn't work out how Jack had vanished so quickly. 'Come out, you little mongrel!' Ernest pulled his mask down around his neck, the better to shout. That was when Jack got a good look at him. 'If you don't come out, I'll kill you.'

Despite his throbbing head, Jack noted the absurdity of this threat. With a grunt of annoyance, Ernest took one last look, and pulled his horse round.

Jack lay still for a moment, hardly daring to believe he had escaped. Then suddenly he realized that it was not sweat trickling into his eyes, but blood. He put his hand to his head and discovered a deep cut in his scalp. He stood up gingerly and peered over the lip of the hole. The first thing he saw was the two bushrangers galloping off fast. The next was his family running towards him. He struggled to climb out of the pit which had saved his life.

Crowing with triumph and brandishing the bag full of valuables, Jack limped to meet them. Rebecca shrieked at the blood trickling down Jack's face. Hugging him fiercely and whirling him around in relief, she scolded him for being so foolhardy. Lucy and Luke looked on with smiles of relief.

The coach pulled in to Jericho. The driver leapt down and strode towards the police watchhouse bawling, 'We've been robbed. We've been robbed. Two bushrangers jumped us. They got the mail! We've been robbed!'

The Greenwoods dismounted and looked around. Jericho was a shanty town of tents and mud-and-bark huts which had sprung up overnight when gold had been discovered. The only buildings of any permanence were the watchhouse, a stables and a general store. Rebecca was appalled at the mud and squalor. Luke put his arm around her shoulders. Jack and Lucy looked around inquisitively.

The coach driver returned with a policeman. Assistant-Commissioner Danks seemed to be all bustle and bother.

'Where did it happen?' he inquired breathlessly.

'Just this side of Jindabyne Creek,' the driver replied.

Danks seemed to be unsure of what to do next. He glanced

at the new arrivals as if for inspiration. 'This is outrageous. Something will have to be done about this. Yes, indeed. Oh yes.'

It was clear, even to Jack and Lucy, that Danks was in a job too big for him.

Picking up their meagre baggage, the Greenwoods set off up the muddy thoroughfare which served as the main street.

'It is insufferable, Officer. Law-abiding people should be able to travel unmolested on Her Majesty's highways,' said Luke as they moved away, their boots squelching in the ubiquitous slush.

'We must get something to eat and drink,' Luke declared.

'And find a doctor to look at Jack's head,' added Rebecca. She eyed the make-shift, tumbledown dwellings with misgiving. 'It's ... not quite what I thought it would be.'

Her husband smiled with a mixture of reassurance and apology. But Lucy and Jack did not share their mother's misgivings about their new surroundings. The ramshackle town and the diggers and their families in their outlandish clothes looked exciting.

A tough boy, a bit older than Jack and with a larrikin look about him, observed Jack's limp. 'Hey, Hoppy, why don't you learn how to walk properly!' he jeered.

Jack blushed, but, as he turned to face him, Lucy plucked at his sleeve. 'Come on, Jack, don't take any notice.'

The young tough pointed at Jack's bandage. 'Like your hat, Hoppy.' Lucy had to drag Jack away. Jack glared back at the tough as the family arrived in front of the only building which showed any sign of prosperity, a store.

They were now at the top of a hill and from this vantage

point they could look down to see the whole of the goldfields. The shanty town was perched on the banks of a wide river. It looked as though a giant mole had been furrowing the land. There were pits and mullock-heaps and piles of tailings everywhere. Smoke wisped up into the frigid sky.

They walked up the steps of the store, a sign proclaiming it to be 'Lovejoy's General Store'. As their eyes adjusted to the gloom they made out the owner of the store at the far end of the counter.

No more inappropriate name could have been chosen for him: Mr Lovejoy was a lean, gloomy man, dressed all in black. There was an unmistakable air of malice about him that gave him the look of a preacher who has swapped his allegiance from God to the Devil.

This impression was reinforced by his present activity. On a perch was the oddest-looking bird the Greenwoods had ever seen. They learnt later that it was called a tawny frog-mouthed owl. Lovejoy was feeding it a mouse. Jack and Lucy shuddered as the wriggling tail slowly disappeared into the mouth of the eerie creature which then blinked its spooky amber eyes as if in thanks.

'Was that nice, Jasper? Did that taste good?' doted Lovejoy, as he stroked the bird's tawny plumage. The man turned and confronted the Greenwoods.

'We would like to buy something to eat,' Luke said. Lovejoy nodded as he eyed them up and down with disdain. 'But first, I'd like to explain a little problem we have. You see, we've just been robbed and we were hoping that you could ... trust us until we ... find some gold.'

There was a deafening silence as Lovejoy and the bird stared witheringly at their customers.

'*Trust* you?' the shopkeeper hissed. Lovejoy's voice and his glittering eyes reminded Jack of a snake.

'We've always paid our debts. Believe me,' Luke said.

'Believe you!' The family began to wilt as Lovejoy's true character revealed itself. 'Not one person in Jericho is worthy of trust, Sir. Why should you be any different?'

Luke and Rebecca were overwhelmed by this odious man; and the sinister look in his cruel eyes made Jack and Lucy want to turn and run from the shop.

'But I am not a hard man. My heart is not so stony that it is not moved by the sight of hungry young mouths.' He bent down close to Jack and Lucy. When he was trying to be nice he was even more abhorrent than when he was being nasty. They shrank back. 'I see your wife has a most beautiful brooch she might like to sell me.' His eyes lit up as he gazed at it covetously.

Luke unhooked his watch from its fob. 'How much would you give me for this?'

'Oh, that's just a watch. My main interest is precious stones and jewellery.' Small flecks of spittle appeared on his lips as he relished these words. 'Perhaps twenty-five shillings?'

'It's worth much more than that.'

'Beggars can't be choosers.'

Luke realized he would get no further. 'I think it is time to go, Rebecca, children.' He ushered them to the door.

Lovejoy's eyes narrowed as he watched them go. 'Just a moment, Sir. Haven't I seen you somewhere before?' he inquired.

'I don't think so. Good day.'

The Greenwoods filed out.

Lovejoy turned to Jasper. 'I didn't like them very much, Jasper, my friend, and I'm sure I've seen him somewhere before.'

Jasper leaned forward in expectation as Mr Lovejoy picked up another dead mouse and fed it into the owl's gaping mouth.

The Greenwoods paused indecisively outside the store.

'Dad, I'm hungry,' Lucy complained.

Luke called to a passing digger, 'Excuse me, Sir. Does Jericho have a doctor?'

The digger looked pityingly at the naïve arrivals. 'You could try Doc Slope. That place over there.' They followed his pointing hand to where a rough-and-ready mud hut stood.

'Thank you,' Luke said.

'Good luck ... You'll need it,' the digger smirked as he plodded away.

The man who answered the door was dressed in a grubby white suit. A battered panama hat was crammed on to his head. He was unshaven and unkempt. The Greenwoods were used to a more respectable sort of doctor in Melbourne and wondered whether they had come to the right dwelling.

'Are you Doctor Slope?'

'I sure am, and I am delighted to make your acquaintance, Sir.' Doc spoke in a Mississippi drawl, thick enough to cut with a knife.

Luke introduced himself and his family.

'And this must be the reason for your visit,' Doc said, looking at Jack's bandaged head. 'Just step on in and I'll have a look at it, young man.'

They entered the Doctor's ramshackle abode. Inside was

a chaos of bottles, boxes, jars, tins and all the paraphernalia of an apothecary and doctor, and a very untidy one at that.

Doc's living conditions and appearance were misleading: his doctoring was deft and sure. Gently, he removed Jack's improvised bandage and inspected the wound.

'Uhuh, uhuh. Allow me to compliment you, Ma'am and Sir, on the strong skull bones you have given your little ones. I do believe it would take a pick to harm this fine cranium.'

'I'm afraid I can't take credit for that, Doctor. Jack's father died two years ago,' Luke said.

'I'm mighty sorry to hear that, Ma'am.'

Rebecca smiled and shrugged. 'It was fever. But I've been very lucky since.' She looked at Luke. There was no doubt what she meant.

'I notice from your accents you're British. Were the youngsters born in England?'

'John and I came to Australia when they were tots. But Luke's only been here a couple of years.' Rebecca and Luke smiled at each other, bemused by the eccentric American.

Doc poured a large glassful of bourbon whiskey and offered it to Jack. 'Could I offer the patient some anaesthetic?' Rebecca declined on Jack's behalf.

'A shame to waste it,' beamed the doctor and tossed it back. He seemed to glow as the spirit flooded through his system and he hummed a Dixie air as he disinfected and dressed Jack's wound.

Lucy glanced around the cluttered room and caught sight of a very odd contraption on a table. 'What's that, Doctor?'

'Now that there, young lady, is what you call a camera, a discovery of the new science and art of photography.

Brought it with me from the United States. Guess it's the only one in this country.'

Lucy nodded and smiled. She was getting used to his explosive manner of talking.

'I guess you've come here to find gold, Sir?' Doc asked.

Luke's voice saddened as he related their ill-fortune.

'Allow me to offer my commiserations on such a terrible stroke of fate.'

'So we're thinking of catching the coach back to Melbourne tomorrow.'

'I'd like to advise against that, Sir. In the goldfields, a man can be free, not only financially free – you can dig up enough in a week to last you a lifetime – but also free from the grip of government. And a lousy British government at that.'

The Greenwoods were almost too tired to move. They looked at the flamboyant doctor with bewilderment.

Luke finally roused himself. 'Thank you so much for your treatment, Doctor. I'm afraid we have no money to pay you.'

'Nor would I accept a red cent from you unfortunate people. I want you to share my humble dwelling tonight. I'll just rustle up some grits for our supper.'

After supper, while the adults were making up something to sleep on, Jack and Lucy sat out on the verandah, staring down on Jericho. The tents were illuminated from within by oil lamps. A hundred cooking fires glowed and winked. Under the veil of night, beneath the star-spattered sky, the settlement looked like an elves' bivouac. Mr Lovejoy's store, tall, angular and ugly like its owner, brooded over the black and stark scene. A crescent moon was beginning its hike up the sky.

Lucy could tell Jack was in a bad mood, she always could. 'It's pretty, isn't it,' she observed.

Jack grunted.

'Isn't Doc Slope nice,' said Lucy.

Jack grunted.

'Does your leg hurt?'

'No.'

'Does your head?'

'No.'

'Why are you cross then?'

'I bet our real father would never have got us into this mess.'

'Don't start that, Jack.'

'Well, he wouldn't. He wouldn't have let them get away with all our money.'

Lucy sighed with exasperation. She had heard it all before.

'Our real father would've been able to do something.'

'Like what?' Lucy asked.

'Luke was scared,' Jack declared emphatically.

'Everybody was.'

'At least I *did* something.'

'And nearly got yourself killed,' snapped Lucy.

Jack looked hurt.

She reached out and touched his hand. 'It was very brave of you to save the rings.'

'I didn't care about the rings. I wanted to save the brooch that Father gave Mother.'

'Honestly, Jack,' said Lucy, exasperated, 'Luke's our father now.'

'Not our real one.'

'Nothing can bring our real one back.'

'At least I haven't forgotten him,' Jack retorted.

It had been a long, hard day for them all. Lucy rounded on her brother with tears welling up in her eyes. 'Nor have I. But Mother loves Luke, and you're just going to have to get used to that.'

'Who wants a father who's a coward,' Jack jeered.

Lucy wanted to say something that would prove to Jack that he was wrong, but she was too distressed. She got up quickly and ran along the verandah, weeping.

Jack stayed where he was, brooding. He, too, was miserable. He loved his father, his real father, still, and, as proof that he would never forget him, he was determined to keep Luke out of his heart. But that meant it was half empty. Now, under the remote stars, with his sister sobbing quietly in the darkness, Jack's heart felt as cold and hollow as an echo.

CHAPTER
TWO

A mopoke sounded mournfully in the night. Ernest and Bones lurked in the trees, waiting. A cart was approaching along the trail. But this time, the bushrangers didn't have their guns drawn, nor were they masked.

'It's him.' They spurred their horses forward.

The driver of the cart was unrecognizable in the gloom but the voice was unmistakable. 'I hope you've got something to pay me with this time,' he hissed.

'Don't worry, Uriah, the pickings were quite rich today, weren't they, Bones?'

Bones grinned doltishly. Ernest took out Luke's chamois money pouch and his wallet. Lovejoy's ears pricked up when the dull clink announced the contents of the pouch to be gold coins. He reached out for it, but Ernest gave him Luke's wallet instead.

'You'll find enough in there for the provisions, Uriah. Load them up, Bones.' As Bones transferred the bags of stores from the cart to his horse, Lovejoy and Ernest grinned at each other, their teeth flashing in the moonlight.

The next morning was foggy, damp and bone-chilling. Danks' breath turned white in the cold. 'The coach is gone,

I'm afraid,' Danks declared, staring bleakly at the dishevelled family in front of him.

'But it wasn't meant to go until nine o'clock,' Luke said.

'They decided to leave early in case the bushrangers were planning to strike again.'

'When's the next one?' Rebecca asked.

'Next week. I'm afraid there's nothing I can do about it.' Danks gave them a supercilious smile, turned on his heel and strutted back to the watchhouse.

Rebecca stared defeatedly at their uninviting surroundings and shrugged – some inevitable force seemed to be insisting that they stay in Jericho. 'Well, Luke, I'm afraid we're going to have to return to that awful man.'

They gathered up their bags and cases again and trudged miserably up the muddy street. Some of the passers-by looked at them sympathetically, remembering how hard it had been for them to come to terms with the punishing life on the goldfields.

Luke had spent a whole hour bartering their personal effects for the wherewithal to set up camp, but Lovejoy was a merciless bargainer.

'Couldn't you put in another lamp? My watch is a very good one,' Luke pleaded.

Lovejoy glanced at the small pile of valuables on the counter and then at the goods he had traded: a bolt of canvas, some blankets, some rope, a bucket, an axe and an oil lamp. His eyes flicked back and forth calculatingly.

'I've been as generous as I can. In fact, I've allowed my sense of charity to get the better of me. One lamp it is, I'm afraid.' His face mellowed as his eyes rested on Rebecca's brooch again. 'You really should consider selling me that delightful piece. I would make it well worth your while.'

'Mum, don't!' Jack said with alarm.

Rebecca stilled him with a reassuring look. 'I'm sorry, Mr Lovejoy, this brooch has great sentimental value for me.'

'Sentiment doesn't fill your stomachs, does it?' Lovejoy allowed his mask of civility to slip for a moment. showing the malevolent spirit within. He turned to unlock a steelbound chest. 'You're from the Midlands, aren't you, Mr Greenwood?'

'Yes, I am.'

'Where exactly do you come from?'

Luke shifted uneasily. An apprehensive expression flitted across Rebecca's face.

'Dudley.'

'Now isn't that a coincidence. I had a shop in Dudley years ago.'

Lovejoy was so intent on racking his memory that he didn't notice Jack appear noiselessly behind him. While the shopkeeper was depositing their valuables, Jack's heart missed a beat . . . There was Luke's wallet – in the strongbox!

'Hey, that's not yours. He's got your wallet in there!' he exclaimed to Luke.

Lovejoy slammed the lid down hard.

Luke and Rebecca were nonplussed and gaped at their son.

'The boy's mad. What's he talking about?' shouted Lovejoy.

'He's got your wallet in there. The one the bushrangers took,' Jack shouted back.

'What a wicked son you have, Sir.'

Jasper hunched forward menacingly, in complete accord

with his master's opinion. Luke didn't know what to do. He looked helplessly at Rebecca.

Assistant-Commissioner Danks burst in, having heard the raised voices.

'He's a thief,' declared Jack, pointing at Lovejoy.

'What's all this?' Danks demanded.

For a few seconds, the focus of attention had shifted from Lovejoy. He opened the chest noiselessly and palmed the evidence out of sight under the counter.

'Can I be of assistance, Mr Lovejoy?'

Lovejoy did his best to impersonate an honest man. 'They've accused me of stealing a wallet...'

'It's in there,' interrupted Jack. 'Open it up and see for yourself!'

Danks tried to intimidate Jack by advancing on him threateningly. 'Now look here, young man, Mr Lovejoy is a respectable citizen...'

'Oh, let the wretched child have his way,' Lovejoy conceded grandly. He threw open the lid and invited everybody to look inside. 'Is there anything of yours in here, Mr Greenwood?'

Luke shook his head.

Jack couldn't believe his eyes. The wallet was gone.

'If you're satisfied, Sir, I think we can declare the matter closed,' said Danks.

Lovejoy patted Jasper's feathers with a smug smile. Luke was embarrassed by the ugly incident his stepson had caused. He looked at Rebecca in confusion.

Doc led the way up the steep slope, carrying the bolt of canvas. The Greenwoods trudged behind him with their bags

26

and the other goods purchased from Lovejoy. Jack shot a resentful look at Luke. He blamed him, in a twisted way, for what had just happened. The boy was caught painfully between the unhealing memory of his dead father and the galling reality of the man who had replaced him.

Doc came to a halt. 'Now this is a good place. It's higher than the surrounding land, so the water will run off.'

'Once again we are in your debt, Doctor,' Luke smiled.

'I'm just pleased that you decided to stay on. That's reward enough for me.'

Rebecca looked around at the squalid encampment and smiled weakly.

'Now I must return to my surgery. It's time for my next dose of medicine.' Doc's huge wink left little doubt as to what form his medicine would take. He bowed gallantly and ambled back down the street, whistling and swinging his silver-topped cane.

The family set about making a temporary shelter. Rebecca and Luke laid out the canvas and cut it up into equal lengths while the children held it down. Jack shinned expertly up two trees and belayed a rope between them, to be supported in the middle by a centre-pole. They draped lengths of canvas over the rope and fastened them to pegs in the ground with guy-ropes. This teamwork was good for them: it took their minds off their recent misfortunes.

They were soon able to stand back and admire their handi-work. It hadn't been as difficult as they had feared.

A youth, a little older than Jack, sauntered up and joined them in their perusal. Jack and Lucy looked at him inquisitively.

'I'll give you a hand for a shilling,' he offered airily.

'I'm afraid we have no money to spare,' Luke replied.

'Anyway, we're nearly finished,' snapped Jack. The youth's casual manner irritated him.

'What are you going to sleep on?' asked the youth.

The others looked at each other. What indeed?

'You can owe me the shilling. Come on, we need saplings.' He picked up the axe and moved off towards a stand of young eucalyptus. Jack and Lucy followed. With a few accurate strokes the youth chopped down a sapling.

He watched Jack approach. 'You hurt your leg?'

'No,' Jack bristled.

'Why are you limping?'

'I just do.'

'Fair enough. My name's Sean. What's yours?'

They told him.

There was a cry of frustration. A guy-rope had got away from Luke and one side of the tent had collapsed. He was charging around ineffectually after the flapping canvas.

'First time your dad's done it, is it?'

'He's not my father,' Jack snapped. Lucy stepped on his toe.

Sean looked at them quizzically. Behind his happy-go-lucky manner, he was a shrewd young man. 'I heard about you and Lovejoy. He won't forget that in a hurry.'

'I don't care. He's crooked. And that policeman wasn't much use.'

'They're mates. Danks does whatever Lovejoy says.' Sean chopped at another sapling, his action lending vehemence to his words. 'It's not right.'

When they had felled and trimmed enough saplings, they ferried them back to the tent. By lashing them together, they were able to form a frame, and over it they slung canvas to act as a mattress. Sean also helped them build a fireplace of river stones.

Evening was drawing on as they finished their work.

'Well, I'd better be going,' Sean said.

'Thanks for all your help, Sean.'

'Don't forget you owe me a bob,' he grinned. 'I'll see you tomorrow.'

Jack and Lucy smiled as Sean strolled off.

'We'll pay you as soon as we find some gold,' Luke called after him. This statement hung in the air more as a wish than a possibility.

After a meal of hard biscuits, tinned beef and lots of sweet black tea, Luke and Rebecca tucked the children into bed. They had no sheets, and the wool of the blankets rasped against their chins and faces. Rebecca heard their prayers then left them to doze. She and Luke stood in the lamp-light and surveyed their primitive, draughty shelter. They smiled ruefully and Luke held his arm out for Rebecca.

Jack observed this through half-closed eyes as he slipped into sleep, hoping he would not meet there, as he did most nights, sad dreams of his father, to be followed by a sadder awakening without him.

Many miles away, over the rugged hilly country deep in the bush, stood a rough timber hut. It was set into a hillside and well hidden, except at night when the light from a single window spilled out. This light was thrown by a huge fire burning in a crudely made fireplace. The firelight danced brightly on a pile of gold guinea pieces and just as brightly on Ernest's greedy eyes. In the chimney corner, Bones sat crocheting a brightly coloured shawl. This incongruous pastime took his mind off his less gentle activities, and he smiled contentedly to himself.

The bushrangers' den was full of the fruits of their highway robberies. Bags, cases, portmanteaux and wallets of all shapes and sizes were strewn everywhere.

'I wonder if he had any more,' Ernest grunted.

Bones was unable to drag himself away from his soothing handicraft.

'Maybe we should pay him a little visit. Make him turn out his other pocket.'

'Let him keep the rest. They'll need it,' Bones murmured.

'You worry me, Bones. I sometimes wonder whether you're cut out for this life.'

'I reckon we cleaned them out,' Bones observed.

Ernest stared into the fire, recalling the day. He reached down to his belt and unsheathed a large knife. He began to trim his nails. 'There's another thing, too. That brat might've seen my face.'

'He's just a kid, Ernie.'

'His word could still put a noose around my neck.'

'Just forget about him.'

'He made us look stupid. I didn't like that.' Ernest's eyes smouldered in his unshaven, villainous face. He suddenly plunged the knife into the table and there it quivered, making the reflected firelight yaw crazily around the room.

Bones sighed at his partner's viciousness and continued to crochet.

Rebecca and Luke were by now asleep. Perhaps their rest would not have been so quiet if they could have read Mr Lovejoy's black thoughts.

30

'Jasper, my lovely, I do remember that Greenwood fellow from somewhere.'

The bird blinked slowly as if in agreement.

Lovejoy picked over the trinkets and jewellery in his strongbox gloatingly. He fingered Lucy's locket and unclipped the lid. A tiny musical-box inside played a nursery tune. The haunting melody reminded Lovejoy of his own childhood; his eyes clouded as he recalled his earlier years, when his future was full of possibility and richer by far than the life he led now, despite his wealth. The poignant tune had jogged his memory. Suddenly everything came flooding back. It had been about ten years ago, back in England; the workers at the potteries in Dudley had rioted because the owners wanted to reduce their wages. There had been a night of flames, shattering glass, screaming and gunfire. And Mr Lovejoy saw again a younger Luke Greenwood as plain as day, leading the rebellious workers.

'I knew he was a criminal. Didn't I tell you, Jasper, my lovely? Assistant-Commissioner Danks will hear of this!' He kissed the bird on the head, grabbed his cloak and, with a caper of delight, left the shop.

Jasper didn't understand any of this. What he did understand, however, was a scurry of tiny claws by the flour barrels. With a single flap of his wings, he glided down and caught the terrified mouse. He flicked the little creature up in the air and caught it in his beak. Then Jasper swallowed it whole, still struggling and squeaking.

CHAPTER THREE

The first thing Jack saw when he awoke was the small plaque his father had given him before he died. On it was carved BLESS THIS HOUSE. Jack had nailed it up on the centre-pole of their tent.

His mother handed him a steaming bowl of porridge. 'No milk, I'm afraid, children.'

'Doesn't matter,' Lucy lied.

Luke sat on his sapling-bed, eating, beside him a spade and a prospecting dish. 'I'm going down to the river to try my luck,' he announced. 'Do you want to come?'

The children certainly did. All they had to do was pull on their boots. They thoroughly approved of the goldfields custom of sleeping in their clothes.

The sky had cleared and the sun, still low in the sky, had no thunderclouds to overcome. Their breath smoked in the frosty air. The atmosphere was crisp and dry, not water-logged as it had been for the past days.

'Now you must do exactly what your father tells you.' Lucy and Jack nodded quickly, dying to be on their way. Rebecca kissed them goodbye.

Just then, they all became aware that an old Chinaman was standing watching them. He wore a threadbare silk jacket, a coolie hat, baggy trousers tied at the knees, and rope sandals. He had a long pigtail down his back.

'Hello. My name is Lin Ping. I live just over there.' He pointed to the next encampment. His voice had a sing-song intonation and he could not say his 'l's. They sounded more like 'r's, so 'Lin' came out sounding more like 'Rin'.

'Our name is Greenwood. We're pleased to meet you.'

'I am also pleased and honoured,' said Lin, bowing deeply. For a moment, the Greenwoods and Lin stared good-naturedly at one another, not sure how to continue.

Lin pointed down the hill. 'Come, I show you good place in river,' he offered, leading the way.

Rebecca returned to the tent and set about making it more comfortable. Her eyes rested for a moment on the carved wooden plaque. But, with a shake of her head, she banished the ghosts of yesterday and began to tidy up.

As Lin, Jack, Lucy and Luke walked along the riverbank, they passed thirty or so diggers going about the arduous business of gold-seeking. Some were panning at the river's edge, some were using a Californian cradle, and those sinking shallow shafts a short distance from the river were using puddling tubs. The Greenwoods looked around eagerly and Luke greeted everyone with friendliness. The diggers observed the newcomers silently, seeming to say, 'You'll learn to save all your energy for what really matters, gold-digging.' Luke finally took up his position some distance from the others, so as not to encroach on their claims in any way.

'I hope you have much luck,' Lin said as he bowed and took his leave. So pleasant had he been, Luke and the youngsters were sorry to see him go.

Squatting down on the shingly bank. Luke tried to do what

the other diggers were doing. Now and then, he sneaked a sideways glance to see if his technique was correct. His first efforts were clumsy. There was no doubt about it: he had a lot to learn.

The youngsters quickly tired of watching this repetitious process. 'Can we go along the bank a bit, please?'

Luke looked at the docile, smooth-flowing river. It seemed quite safe. 'Don't wander too far, and keep away from the edge,' said Luke, reluctantly.

Lucy and Jack set out. The youngsters had, of course, seen bush on the outskirts of Melbourne, but nothing as wild, untouched and thick as this. As the sun hit the ground and foliage, a smell of herb and flower and earth rose up. Jack and Lucy smiled at each other with sheer enjoyment at the new sights and sounds. A flock of rosellas took off in a cloud, flying in tight formation and scolding the intruders. A troop of wallabies disappeared down a slope, jumping like huge grass-hoppers.

Presently, the children arrived at a giant old gum tree which overhung the river.

'Wow, what a beauty!' Jack exclaimed. He ran to it and shinned up it. Perhaps in compensation for his broken gait on the ground, he had an uncanny ability for tree climbing. 'Hey, Lucy, come on up, it's great!'

Lucy gingerly climbed up and joined her brother who was balancing recklessly on an enormous branch which spread over the river.

'Wouldn't it be great for a tree-hut?' exclaimed Jack.

Lucy nodded. From their vantage point they could see for miles around: the river, with the diggers along it working away; then the clearing in which Jericho itself stood; and beyond that the bush, stretching olive-green and vast to the distant mountains.

'It's pretty up here,' Lucy said.

But Jack ignored his sister. 'Ideal for a tree-hut.'

They let the sun beat down on their backs to banish the dampness they'd soaked up during the past rains. They were startled by a pair of magpies who noticed them and swooped low over the river, gossiping loudly.

They dropped to the ground, to be confronted by two cut-throat-looking toughs. Jack recognized one as the boy who had jeered at him the day before, a ragamuffin called Ted.

'Well, if it isn't old Hoppy.'

Jack coloured with anger but held his peace, realizing that not only was he outnumbered, but both boys were bigger than he was.

'Do you know where you are?' said Ted, prodding him in the chest.

Jack shook his head. Lucy was very frightened.

'You're on our territory. That tree's ours.'

Jack, plucking up his courage, retaliated, 'I can't see your name on it.'

'I think we're going to have to teach this fellow a lesson,' Ted said to Bobby, his friend. 'Listen to me, you're trespassing on our land and you're going to have to be punished.'

Jack and Lucy licked their dry lips.

Ted looked from one to the other. 'This your girlfriend?'

'She's my sister.'

'What's your name?'

'Lucy Greenwood.'

'What's yours, Hoppy? You'd better answer me.'

'Jack Sharp.'

Ted and Bobby exchanged a puzzled look. 'You can't be brother and sister if your name's Sharp and her name's Greenwood. Are you fibbing, Hoppy?' Ted poked him in the chest again. This was too much for Jack, who launched himself at Ted. Ted was easily the stronger and began to gain the upper hand.

Lucy, so pleasant and serene when not aroused, gave a shriek like a war-cry and hurled herself on top of Ted, her small fists flailing. 'Leave him alone, you big bully. Leave him!'

Bobby tried to drag her off but earned an elbow in the ribs for his trouble. He doubled up but was still able to clamp a hand on her wrist and tug.

Things looked bad until Sean jogged up in his unhurried way. 'Why don't you fight someone your own size, Ted?' He pulled Ted off. 'Like me, for example.'

Ted was furious but had no stomach for a scrap with Sean. 'Who asked you to stick your nose in?'

'You know me, Ted. Never wait to be asked.'

'This is our territory,' Bobby chipped in.

'We don't mind sharing,' Sean taunted.

'Let's leave Sean to play with these two girls.' The bullies slunk off. When they were at a safe distance, Ted screamed back, 'You'll regret this, Hoppy. And you too, Sean.'

'Never knows when to quit, does our Ted,' Sean said.

Jack fingered his eye, which was already beginning to darken and swell. He picked twigs and dirt out of his skinned knees – but he was smiling, because he knew it was not just Lucy and him against the world, it was them *and* Sean now.

'If you have any more trouble just give us a shout,' said Sean, as he sauntered away, his hands in his pockets.

Jack dunked his head in the cold river water. The throbbing went away for a moment. When he pulled it out, though, the pain returned.

'Perhaps you ought to go and see Doc Slope,' suggested Lucy. Jack shook his head. 'There's no shame in being beaten by somebody bigger than you.' Lucy knew that was what was on his mind.

'He didn't beat me,' Jack retorted untruthfully.

Lin Ping approached them along the riverbank, his prospecting dish slung over his back. 'Hello, little ones.'

Jack was going to smile at his accent, but his sore cheek stopped him.

'Ah, Jack, sore eye. Must come with me. I fix.' Without further ado, he grabbed Jack's hand and led him off. Jack was surprised at the strength in the old man's grasp.

All the way home, Lin chatted on. Lucy and Jack understood some, but not all, of it. Lin seemed very glad to have somebody to talk to.

He ushered the children into his yard. They were surprised to see that a neat vegetable garden took up most of the space. Lin revived the fire in the outside hearth and put the kettle on. He disappeared into his hut. Lucy and Jack looked at the garden inside the neat enclosure. There were rows of cabbages, onions, carrots, peas and beans.

Lin returned with what looked like a jar full of dried grass. He put it inside a piece of linen and poured hot water over it. 'This will stop eye from swelling. Hurt bit, then no more.' He gently applied the hot compress to the puffy purple cheekbone. Jack winced but slowly all the smarting disappeared. 'You walk into tree?' Lin cackled at his own joke.

'I wish I could have bashed him up.'

Lin nodded understandingly and looked at Lucy. She shrugged. 'I wish I could bash everybody up who called me names.'

'And what would this do?'

'Make them stop,' Jack replied.

'But it would make them call you more names.'

'Then I'd bash them up again.'

Lin dipped the herbs into the hot water again and repositioned it on Jack's cheek. 'It is better to do nothing, then evil people go away.'

'Then they'd think you were scared. My father told me not to let anyone think you're scared.'

Lin had seen enough of Luke for this to puzzle him. 'Luke said that?'

'No, my real father. Luke is scared.'

'It is often stronger to avoid a fight than to fight.'

'That's being a coward.'

Lin did not reply but smiled and shook his head. He dropped the compress back into the dish.

'Jack, the swelling's gone down.' Lucy cried. Jack grinned.

Lin looked up at the sky, thinking, in a way the children would become used to as they got to know him better. 'In my belief, we say evil of your attacker will turn against him.'

Jack chose not to understand this and there was a silence.

'You do not believe me?'

Jack shrugged.

Lin stood. 'I will show you. Run at me and hit me!'

Jack rose, looking rather bewildered. He made no move.

'Run towards me and hit me. Come!'

Jack sheepishly complied. Using what looked to the children like some odd dance step, Lin avoided Jack's charge. Jack almost fell over. He looked confused.

'Now try again, but harder.' Jack charged, but with much more determination. Once again Lin evaded and blocked him. Jack overbalanced, falling to the ground.

Lin helped him up. 'You see, evil intention of attacker will hurt him more than ever you can.'

Jack looked back at the old Chinaman with new respect. He noticed for the first time how lined and wrinkled his ancient face was. It was hard to tell whether he was laughing or frowning, but Lucy and Jack agreed, when they discussed it later on the way home, that he had probably done a great deal of both in his life.

Luke was not doing very well. He still hadn't mastered the knack of swilling out the sand and silt with successive scoops of water and allowing the heavier particles, possibly gold-dust, to collect at the bottom. So intent was he, he did not hear Danks sidle up with a mixture of furtiveness and fear. Danks had, after all, been told that Luke was a dangerous criminal. 'I know who you are,' Danks declared quaveringly.

The sudden announcement startled Luke. He looked at Danks, puzzled. 'Of course you do. I told you when I made a statement about the bushrangers.'

'But I know who you really are and why you left England.'

Luke was appalled. He was convinced he had left his past behind. He waited for Danks to continue, but Danks just buffed the brass buttons of his uniform with his cuff. To cover his guilty confusion, Luke reached for his spade to lay back a deeper level of shingle.

Danks stepped back in alarm. 'Don't do anything rash, Mr Greenwood. Remember, I'm an officer of the crown.'

Luke decided to brazen it out. 'Officer Danks. I would like to stop and chat but I've got work to do.'

'Can I see your mining licence?'

'My what?'

'Your miner's licence.'

'I didn't know you had to have one.'

'Didn't know! Didn't know! Everybody knows. Unless you procure one by Monday I will have to arrest you.'

'How much do they cost?'

'Thirty shillings . . . every month . . .'

Luke gasped. They hadn't as much as thirty pennies to their name at the moment.

'You'll have to stop until you get one. Is that understood?'

Luke gathered up his spade and dish, and returned home defeated.

Rebecca tried to console her dejected husband.

'Why so much?' she asked.

'It's the law.'

'We'll have to find it somehow.'

'We haven't got enough to go back to Melbourne, or enough to stay here,' sighed Luke. Rebecca placed a comforting hand on his shoulder, but Luke had even graver news. 'I'm afraid Lovejoy has told Danks about my past.'

Rebecca grimaced, her worst apprehensions confirmed. 'But you've paid your penalty. He can't do anything now.'

'I hope not.'

Luke stared around at their new home. It would be a great

shame if their fresh start was ruined by something that was over and done with.

'What will we do?'

Rebecca was stronger than Luke in some ways and more realistic about facing unpleasant facts. She fingered her brooch. 'We will have to sell this to the horrid Mr Lovejoy.'

'No!'

'It's the only way, Luke.'

'Jack will be upset. He'll see it as a betrayal of his father.'

'I'll talk to him. He'll understand.'

'Will he?'

'He'll have to.' Rebecca knew her son had sensitivities, but the survival of the family had to come first.

So effective had Lin's herbal remedy been, that neither Rebecca nor Luke had noticed anything amiss with Jack's eye. That night, as Jack and Lucy sat on their beds with blankets draped over them to keep out the cold, it seemed as though a storm was brewing. Icy gusts made the tent balloon and flap. Luke was outside checking the ropes and pegs.

Rebecca was reading to them from their favourite book, *The Old Curiosity Shop* by Charles Dickens. '... night, when the noise of every strange machine was aggravated by the darkness; when the people near them looked wilder and more savage, when bands of unemployed labourers paraded the road, or clustered by torch light around their leaders who told them, in stern language, of their wrongs, and urged them on to frightful cries and threats, when maddened men armed with sword and fire brand, spurning the tears and prayers of women who would restrain them, rushed forth on errands of terror and destruction, to work no ruin half so surely as their own ...'

Rebecca's tone became more emotional as she realized how closely these happenings resembled that fateful part of her own husband's past.

'Did this happen in England?' Jack inquired.

'Yes, it did, Jack.'

'Why?'

'Because the workers were getting poorer and poorer and they couldn't stand it any longer.'

'Why didn't they do something about it?' Lucy asked.

'They tried, but soldiers came with guns and killed some of them.' She frowned as she recalled the bloody industrial unrest which made so many English people seek kinder lands.

The youngsters went quiet, sensing that the passage she had just read meant a lot more to her than she would let on.

Jack's eyes narrowed as he noticed something different about his mother.

'Mum, you've lost your brooch.'

'No, Jack, I haven't lost it.'

'Where is it?'

'I've had to sell it.'

'Sell it!'

'We need a licence to dig for gold and it costs a lot of money,' Rebecca replied soothingly.

'Why couldn't we sell something else? Something of Luke's?'

'That will do. I didn't want to but we had to.'

'But Father gave it to you.'

Luke entered the tent to hear the last remark. Rebecca cautioned him to keep out of it with a gesture. Jack scowled at Luke and pushed past him into the night. Luke made to follow but Rebecca shook her head. 'Leave him alone for a while.'

Lucy frowned. She hated it when Jack destroyed their feeling of being a family. It made all their other setbacks look small when they felt they belonged to each other; but just as this was happening, Jack seemed to shatter it on purpose. As if to underline how easily he threatened their precarious happiness, the lamp flickered and guttered and went out.

Outside, the storm was gathering in force and huge drops of rain suddenly slapped on to the canvas. How long would her brother choose to remain outside in the cold, Lucy wondered, when they all wanted him inside with them. The chilly winds, which so easily penetrated the flimsy structure, seemed to blow straight through Lucy's heart.

Lovejoy set his face against the driving sleet and made for the watchhouse. With the strong gusts plucking at his cape, he resembled a flapping bird of prey.

He entered and shook off the rain. Danks rolled his eyes in exasperation – he knew what was coming.

'Our precious Mr Greenwood still enjoys the freedom of the town, I notice.'

'I've told you, Mr Lovejoy, we have no proof that he is who you say he is.'

'I saw him with my own eyes, leading the mob. Then he attacked a soldier and beat him half to death.'

Danks pondered what was best to do. If in doubt, resort to paperwork, was his tried and trusty remedy for all occasions. He pulled a sheet of paper and an inkwell towards him. 'What we will do is write out a special report and send it to Melbourne. They will contact the British authorities. If he is the man you say he is, I will bring the full weight of the law down on him.' This was one of Danks' favourite expressions and he rolled it round his mouth once again. 'The full weight of the law.'

Lovejoy smirked approvingly.

So fierce had the storm been, that Jack and Lucy had been driven from their camp beds early to go for a warming walk. Because today was Sunday, not even the most industrious of diggers were working. Sunday was a day of rest and worship, 'the wash-and-mend day'.

Lucy put her hand on Jack's arm, motioning him to listen. There it was again.

'What is it?' Jack wondered.

'Sounds like a drum and bugle.'

'A drum!'

The riddle was soon solved. A sideshow caravan crested a hill and headed down the slope into Jericho. A draughthorse clad in gaudy livery drew it towards the youngsters. On the driving platform sat a man and a girl, aged about thirteen. He beat a large bass drum with one hand and she blew a bugle. He was wearing a multicoloured topcoat and garish trousers. The girl was dressed in spangled tights and a silk jerkin. Children from the diggings ran happily alongside the caravan as it moved through the settlement.

The man began shouting out with a foreign accent. Lucy was positive it was a French accent. '*Allez! Allez! Allez!* Come along to Marcel's world-famous circus. See him catch bullets in his teeth! Hear him read people's minds, discovering their darkest secrets. Come and wonder at the world's youngest ventriloquist. See her defy death as knives are hurled at her.

Only threepence for children, sixpence for adults. *Allez! Allez! Allez!'*

On the side of the caravan was painted the legend 'MARVELLOUS MARCEL, MESMERIST AND ILLU-SIONIST. CLEOPATRE, VENTRILOQUIST'. The vehicle came to a halt in the large clear area in front of the watch-house.

Sean sauntered up and greeted Jack and Lucy. Together they watched the man and the girl set up the sideshow. Marcel and Cleopatre unloaded canvas walls and spread them between poles to provide an enclosure. Cleopatre glanced curiously at the tattered youngsters. When they caught her looking, she pointedly ignored them as if they were of no interest to her.

An old lady had set up a rickety old stall from which she was selling home-made sweets, toffee apples and gingerbread men.

'Got any money, Sean?'

'Sixpence.'

'Those sweets look mighty good.' They walked over and bought a bag of sticky lollies.

Doc Slope had opened a booth from which he was selling his famous ointment and elixir. The children stopped and listened for a while, chewing noisily on the sweets.

'Let me assure you, ladies and gentlemen, that Doctor Slope's Patented Ointment and Elixir for Man and Beast will cure everything: blisters, cuts, ringworm, heat-rash. If you or your horse get saddle sores, it will cure you both. And the miserable price I'm asking is only one and sixpence. That's right, just eighteen pennies.'

Doc winked hugely at the youngsters as they ambled back

to the sideshow. Marcel was thumping the drum in front of the canvas enclosure which Cleopatre was struggling to erect.

'If we give you a hand, will you let us in for free?' Sean asked.

Cleopatre stared at them appraisingly. 'That's ninepence.'

Sean bridled at her coolness. 'I can count, too.'

'Will I get ninepence worth of work out of you?'

'I'll work hard,' said Lucy eagerly.

Cleopatre smiled at her sincerity. 'All right.'

The children were glad of the exercise because the day was bitterly cold.

'*Ma petite*, you must go and get ready. *Vite!*' Marcel shouted.

'Could you finish off here?' Clee smiled and left.

Jack really liked the look of the self-possessed showgirl. In fact, such a liking had he taken to her, he was absolutely terrified during the first routine, a knife-throwing act. Marcel had shown the crowd how sharp the knives were – their points were like needles. Cleopatre stood calmly against a wooden panel. Her slim body was outlined by the splintered puncture-marks of previous performances. She now had heavily rouged cheeks and kohl around her eyes. She stared fearlessly at her father. Jack could scarcely bear to look. With a whistle the first knife thudded into the board, inches from her neck-pulse. Then another and another until all ten knives quivered in the wood. Cleopatre stepped forward and curtseyed to the clapping audience.

Her perils were far from over. For the next trick, she lay down inside a wooden trunk that was brightly decorated with moons and stars.

Marcel picked up six swords and slashed them through the air. 'How can my precious daughter escape death? Will her young body be pierced with these sharp swords?' He rammed the six swords through the box until they stuck out the other side.

The audience gasped. Lucy grabbed hold of Jack's hand and squeezed it fearfully. But Cleopatre had escaped death again. When her father withdrew the swords and opened the lid, she pranced out as whole as when she had gone in.

But the most horrifying trick of all was when Marcel bound her hand and foot with cord, padlocked her inside a large canvas sack and lowered her into a barrel full of water.

'Each time I ask myself how ... how can I do this to my own daughter? Each time I wonder, will she come out alive?' Marcel shouted.

Jack's heart was in his mouth. The seconds ticked by. He was about to rush to her rescue, when Cleopatre suddenly erupted from the water, brandishing her ropes. Jack clapped until his hands stung.

And that was not the end of her talents. She was also an accomplished ventriloquist. She delighted the crowd by appearing to speak from every section of the enclosure without moving her lips.

The last trick of the afternoon did not involve Cleopatre. Marcel boasted that he could mesmerize anybody and look straight into their souls.

'I need a subject.' He looked around. 'You, Sir. Yes, you. I can see you are a man of great mystery.'

Everybody turned to see who it was. It was Bones. Jack racked his brains. There was something about his overall

47

appearance which was familiar. Jack had seen him somewhere before, but he couldn't remember where.

Bones had been as enthralled as any child by the show and was easily persuaded by the crowd to step forward. Jack had also noticed Mr Lovejoy standing at the back, unsmiling and motionless like some sinister statue. Bones shambled goodnaturedly up to the dais and sat down.

'This won't hurt at all. Look into my eyes, deep into my eyes deep, deep, deep. Good. You are feeling sleepy, very sleepy. You are now under my command.'

Bones, as had become clear by now, was not the brightest of men. He fell under Marcel's spell easily.

'Now I want you to tell me things you have never told anybody else. Secrets you have kept locked up in your mind. Reveal them now.'

Bones replied as if asleep: 'I know where there is a lot of money and treasure.'

'Where is it?' Marcel asked. The audience leaned forward, breathlessly awaiting the answer.

Lovejoy broke the spell by striding forward. 'Stop it! Stop. Stop this sorcery on the Lord's day. It is a sacrilege.'

Marcel turned around, startled. The diggers resented it, too. 'Sit down,' ... 'Let him get on with the show,' they heckled.

'Leave this poor simple soul alone. Such witchcraft is an insult to the Sabbath.' Lovejoy hauled Bones to his feet. Bones was not sure where he was, as Mr Lovejoy bustled him out. The crowd booed angrily.

Then, suddenly, Jack remembered where he'd seen Bones before. He was almost incoherent as he tried to explain the implications to Lucy and Sean. 'Hey, I know who that skinny fellow is. He was one of the bushrangers. I wasn't sure at first because of the mask. And that proves Lovejoy is one of them. Because he knew he was going to spill the beans.'

Sean and Lucy took a moment to digest this, then they nodded their heads.

A mounted policeman sat on his horse under some trees, waiting for the satisfied crowd milling out of the sideshow to disperse. Jack, Lucy and Sean went over to the step of the caravan where Cleopatre sat drying her hair.

'That was great,' said Jack. Cleopatre smiled graciously.

'You must be very brave,' Lucy commented.

'It's just practice really.'

'How come you weren't stabbed by the swords?' asked Jack.

'I know, there's a door in the bottom and you slip out that way,' Sean guessed. Cleopatre shook her head emphatically.

'How else could you do it?' Sean challenged.

'I'm not allowed to tell.'

Cleopatre suddenly jerked her head up. The others could hear the commotion, too. The policeman had dismounted and Marcel was facing him, railing and shaking his fist at him. Cleopatre leapt up and raced over, the other youngsters following in her wake. They heard the policeman say, 'I don't know about that, Sir, but I do have a warrant for your arrest. The magistrate in Melbourne will decide whether the charges are true.'

'What's wrong, Papa?' Cleopatre screamed.

'It is crazy. The tailor in Melbourne says we have not paid him. Of course we have not. We have to earn the money. He knew this. We told him.'

'Well, that is as may be, but I have my orders, so if you wouldn't mind . . .'

'How can I pay this debt if I am in prison?'

'That's not for me to say, Sir.'

All figures of authority were very unpopular on the gold-fields. Several diggers gathered around sympathetically. Cleopatre grasped hold of her father's hand and tried to prevent the policeman from taking him away.

'You can't take my father away. He's done nothing wrong.'

'I'm sorry, Miss. He's broken the law.'

Doc Slope had joined the swelling crowd. Marcel turned to them and, in his best fairground style, delivered an impromptu speech. 'What will become of this country, this beautiful young country, my friends? The creative spirit, which can make people laugh and cry, is to be locked up in a dungeon, all for the sake of a few pennies.'

'Forty-nine pounds ten shillings,' Sergeant Collins interjected mildly. But nobody paid any attention to this detail.

As Marcel got more excited his accent thickened. 'What will become of this country where British justice, from England remember, is allowed to rule this land and its people?'

The diggers mumbled in agreement. 'He is absolutely right. Listen to the wisdom of the man. I say listen.' Doc shook his cane in the air.

'I don't know anything about this, Sir. Please come along to the lock-up with me,' Sergeant Collins said.

Lucy, Jack and Sean listened closely to what Marcel was saying. They only half-understood but instinctively agreed with it. Collins took a firmer hold on Marcel and escorted him to the watchhouse.

'You must throw off the yoke of imperialism, of unfair laws. *Vive la république. Liberté, égalité, fraternité.*'

'Amen, I say, amen to that!' thundered Doc.

'He's right! Justice! It's not fair!' the crowd shouted.

'And what is to become of my sweet daughter while I rot in jail? My poor Cleopatre.'

Cleopatre clung to the policeman's arms, but the weight of her slim body hardly slowed him down at all. He marched on imperturbably to the watchhouse. 'Leave my father alone. Leave him alone,' Cleopatre shrieked.

Jack, Lucy and Sean turned to face the sideshow where not half an hour ago they had been clapping and cheering with delight. The canvas walls seemed to have sagged along with their spirits.

'It just isn't fair,' Sean said. Jack and Lucy nodded.

Luke had been hard at work all day, fashioning a table and chairs; Rebecca had prepared a tasty stew. But the children had no interest in either, so full were their thoughts of Cleopatre and her father.

Rebecca tried to jog them out of their misery. 'Lin gave us the vegetables ... and some oil for the lamp. Isn't that good of him?'

Jack and Lucy didn't respond. All they wanted to talk about was what had happened that day. Jack put down his spoon with a clatter.

'It's not fair! Why should he go to prison?'

'If he has not paid his debts, that's breaking the law,' Luke answered gently.

'The law didn't get the bushrangers,' Jack exclaimed.

'They'll be punished one day.'

Jack gave an unimpressed grunt.

Luke knew he should rebuke him for his rude behaviour

at the table but he also knew that Jack could easily storm out into the night, heralding another evening of silences and glares.

'Mum . . . You know that girl, Cleopatre, can she come and stay with us?

'Stay with us! Lucy dear. we hardly have enough for ourselves.'

'But what will happen to her when her father is put in prison?'

'She'll have to stay with her family or friends.'

'I don't think she's got any.'

'Then she'll have to go to . . . an orphanage,' Rebecca replied sadly.

'But they're horrible places, aren't they?' Jack said.

'Well, it wouldn't be very pleasant staying with us at the moment, Jack. We have nothing.'

Luke had been quiet up till now, listening to his children speak. 'Why do you want her to come and stay?' Luke asked.

'Because we like her. She acts tough, but she's not tough underneath. Not really,' Lucy replied.

The youngsters gazed at their parents imploringly. Rebecca and Luke exchanged a look. Misfortune had toughened them, but it had also disclosed the kindness of strangers like Lin and Doc. Rebecca and Luke accepted that it was their turn, so the chain was forged.

Luke, Jack and Lucy approached the watchhouse. Marcel and Cleopatre huddled around a small fire. On the end of chains bolted into a big tree were manacles, which were closed around Marcel's wrists. Cleopatre nestled under his coat for warmth. They looked around as the Greenwoods

52

walked up. They stared solemnly at one another. Jack could see that Cleopatre's eyes were red from weeping: she tried to smile at Jack, but couldn't.

'Good evening, Sir. My name is Luke Greenwood. My children tell me that you've fallen on hard times.'

Marcel shook his manacles in disgust. 'As you see, Monsieur. I am not worried so much for myself but, for my daughter, it will be very bad.'

'If it would help, she could come to live with us until ... until your fortunes improve.'

Cleopatre did not like the sound of this and clung to her father more tightly.

'But ... but ... Monsieur, why are you so kind to me, a stranger?'

'Well, it seems my children have taken a liking to your daughter ... It's not right for a girl so young to have to fend for herself.'

'Papa ... no ... please ...'

Marcel shushed Cleopatre. Lucy walked up to her and put her hand on her shoulder. 'It's all right. We'll look after you. Honest.'

With a great rattle of chains, Marcel seized Luke's hand and shook it vigorously. 'I will be in your debt eternally. Never have I come across such generosity. I think you must have Norman blood in those English veins, Monsieur Greenwood.' Marcel embraced Cleopatre fiercely. She seemed to be coming to terms with the idea, and the welcoming grins of Jack and Lucy helped quieten her misgivings. Marcel held her at arm's length. 'I will see you soon. *Courage, ma petite. Courage.*'

Luke led his children away beyond the halo cast by the fire

so that father and daughter could take leave of each other. Jack thought it a bit strange that a father who threw daggers at his unflinching daughter every day should have to tell her to have courage; but then he knew, to his cost, that accepting the loss of a father needed a special sort of bravery. Cleopatre hugged her father one last time, then stepped quickly into the darkness where the Greenwoods waited.

CHAPTER FOUR

The gaudy sideshow caravan looked incongruous, parked on the grass behind the Greenwoods' encampment. The cart-horse, Louis, was tethered to its step. Lucy knew it was just her imagination, but it seemed as if the crude paintings of Marcel and Cleopatre on the caravan sides looked less jaunty now.

She saw Cleopatre pulling up handfuls of lush grass and feeding them to the horse. She called out: 'Cleopatra!' She couldn't say it in the French way.

Cleopatre turned to see who it was. She wiped her eyes. Her cheeks were smudged with tears.

Lucy plucked some grass too, and they stood feeding Louis in silence.

'I suppose you miss your father?' Cleopatre nodded. 'My father died of fever two years ago,' Lucy said matter-of-factly.

'But what about . . . ?' Cleopatre began.

'Luke's my stepfather. He's very good to us . . . only Jack can't see it.'

Cleopatre nodded. The girls smiled hesitantly at each other. Louis snorted for more grass.

*

'This foot come back, then this foot and you step and turn.'

Jack tried to follow Lin's instructions. Lin ran at his pupil aggressively. Jack fended him off.

'Good. Good, Jack. Again.' Lin charged at Jack and this time Jack blocked and avoided him much more deftly.

'Yes, yes.' Lin slapped him on the back. 'You not do anything. Let them trip themselves up. Violence punish itself.'

'What do you call this sort of fighting?'

'Not fighting,' Lin scolded. 'Defending only. No word in English. Anyway, not word, but spirit.'

And so Lin continued to teach Jack the basic moves of oriental unarmed combat.

Like all weak and incompetent men in official positions, Danks relished exerting his power over Luke and Rebecca as they stood before him in the watchhouse.

'Now, before I issue you with a miner's licence, I must satisfy myself that you are not a trouble-maker.'

Luke frowned but made no reply.

Danks preened himself against the stiff collar of his uniform. 'Are you a trouble-maker, Mr Greenwood?'

'No.'

'Are you sure?'

'We're both sure,' interjected Rebecca, who was getting angry.

'I'm sure your husband can answer for himself. Now, are you a criminal?'

'I am no criminal.'

'Have you ever been sent to prison?'

Luke began to sweat, despite the cold of the mean little office. He hated dishonesty and had thrashed his children if

56

ever they lied to him, but what else could he do? Without a licence, he couldn't find gold, and without gold his family would starve.

'No.'

'My information is that you have!' Luke looked guiltily at Rebecca. Danks reached for a Bible. 'I want you to swear on this Bible that you are not the same man who led a riot in Dudley, England, some ten years ago and wounded a soldier.'

Luke dropped his eyes and his shoulders slumped in defeat. 'I will not swear on a Bible.'

'I thought not. In that case, I will not issue the licence.' Danks smirked. He could easily see himself in the High Court as a prosecutor sending everybody to the gallows.

By now Rebecca was very angry. She took a step forward. Like all good and courageous women, she had a certain majesty when opposing wrong done to herself or her family. Danks quailed before her sparking eyes. 'I will swear on a stack of Bibles a mile high that I have never been sent to prison. Issue the licence to me.'

'I . . . I . . .' stammered Danks.

'There is the fee. Now issue me the licence.' Rebecca pointed at the thirty shillings on the desk.

Danks was confounded. His court-room assurance had deserted him and he reached for a blank miner's right. Luke looked admiringly at his wife, who smiled, as relieved as he was.

All hands were required on the Greenwoods' claim. Lin and Luke had built a Californian cradle. This was a box with a long upright handle and a race at one end. Paydirt was dumped into the box and water sluiced over it. When it was rocked. the dross was washed out, leaving heavier material behind. Rebecca and Jack took turns at rocking it. Luke ladled water from the river while Lin shovelled the paydirt.

Lucy and Cleopatre were meant to be helping too, but sat on the riverbank talking.

Lin paused and gave Jack a word of advice. 'Do not push too big. Small pushes best. Can keep on all day.' Jack changed his technique. 'Very good. Very good.'

Jack looked askance at the two girls taking their ease on the shingle bank. 'Wish they'd do some work,' he grumbled to his mother.

'Never mind, Jack. Cleopatre is probably missing her father. She needs the company.'

Jack accepted this reluctantly.

Cleopatre and Lucy were getting to know each other. Lucy was picking up scoops of sand in one hand and trickling it through the other.

'Is Cleopatre your real name?' She nodded. 'It sounds hard to say.'

'People call me Clee for short.'

'Clee? It's easier. And you come from France?'

'No, I was born here. But my father came from France.'

'Why did he come to Australia?'

'He was poor in France and hoped he could get rich in Australia.'

'Is your mother from France, too?'

'No, Papa met her here.'

'Is she in Melbourne?'

'Could be. I don't know where she is really. Her and Dad didn't get on. Mum hated moving from town to town with the show. So one trip she stayed behind and when we got

58

back . . . she'd gone . . . for good.' Clee tried to mask the hurt she still felt with a shrug, but it wasn't very convincing.

Lucy continued to dig with her fingers in the sand. Because she was so interested in what was being said, she did not see that she'd uncovered a small rock which glinted dully in the watery sunlight.

'Your father's very funny.' Lucy said.

'He's not really. When he's not in front of a crowd he gets really sad.'

'Why?'

'He misses Mum, I think, and misses where he comes from . . . I mean France. Now he'll miss me.' Clee's voice faltered as she tried to keep back the tears.

Lucy turned away and looked down to see what, to her amazement, looked like a nugget of gold. She was no experienced prospector but she recognized it at once.

'Hey, everybody! Over here! Look what I've found,' she shrieked.

Lovejoy stared gloatingly at the lump of gold on his counter, then raised his eyes sourly to its undeserving owners. He placed the dull-yellow ore on the scales and counterpoised it with weights. Rebecca, Luke and Lin leaned forward expectantly.

'What a lovely piece. Oh, yes. Quite exquisite. Now let me see, the bank rate is' – he made a big show of looking up a printed form – 'three pounds an ounce exactly.'

'Very sorry . . . I think is three pounds three shillings an ounce.'

Lovejoy fixed Lin with a look of utter disdain. 'I charge five per cent commission. Very reasonable, I think. So that is ninety pounds exactly.' He ignored Lin and addressed his comment to the Europeans.

Rebecca and Luke were overjoyed. Lin, however, stepped forward and reached underneath the scales. He removed a large magnet from the underside of the dish the counterweights were on. The gold nugget dipped sharply.

Lovejoy coloured deeply and his voice grew thick with anger. 'Ah, thank you very much. I wondered where that had got to.' He added another counterweight. 'That is ninety-nine pounds.'

'Could we buy back my daughter's musical locket, Mr Lovejoy?' Rebecca asked.

But the shopkeeper had been put into a filthy mood by having to part with so much money. 'No you can't,' he snapped.

Rebecca looked at him for a moment, then shrugged. She would not beg from this odious man. The Greenwoods and the shrewd old Chinaman left the shop, well pleased with their day's work.

Jasper peered up sympathetically at his master, who looked as if he was on the verge of a seizure. Lovejoy's humour was only partly restored when he put the magnet back under the scales ready to rook the next customer.

The heavy rains had held off for a couple of days. Perhaps this signalled the turning of the year. The ground was no longer soggy, so Jack, Clee, Sean and Lucy were able to lie stretched out on the bank underneath their eucalyptus tree, staring into the blue. The air was loud with bird-call. A pair of kookaburras cackled maniacally from the top of the huge tree.

'I reckon we should build a tree-hut,' Jack said.

'Great idea. You're not as silly as you look,' Sean replied. Jack took this amiss until Sean pushed him playfully, and they laughed.

'I thought this was Ted's place,' Lucy said.

'He thinks everything is his,' Sean replied.

'Will he come back?' Lucy asked.

'Let him. He's been getting too big for his boots lately.'

'We'll make a sort of floor with logs.' Jack's mind was alive with plans.

'I'll bring some rope tomorrow,' Sean offered.

'Last one up's a dirty dog,' challenged Jack, leaping to his feet. He scrambled up the tree with his usual ease.

'He must be part-monkey,' commented Sean admiringly.

Had their eyes been sharper or Bojinda's sense of camouflage not so expert, they might have seen the aborigine youth staring at them from the other side of the river. Over his ebony-black body was thrown a wombat-skin cloak. Around his neck were two necklaces of dried seeds. He carried a spear and boomerang, and watched the white youngsters' antics with expressionless interest.

There were many claims on the Greenwoods' new-found wealth. They had borrowed money from Doc Slope which had to be repaid, although he insisted it was a gift. More canvas had to be purchased to repair some storm damage. Luke was also eager to improve their living conditions. He had heard that a family in another encampment was selling up and going back to Melbourne, and was interested in seeing what useful things he could buy from them. Their young daughter had been carried away by fever and they longed to leave the place which had killed her.

The Greenwoods approached the little encampment, which was some distance from their own. Next to the small hut was a stack of freshly milled timber. Further up the hill a man and a woman, their heads bent in prayer, stood beside a freshly dug grave. It was very small, with a wooden cross embedded at its head. There was a bunch of wild flowers laid on the clay.

'Did somebody die?' Lucy asked.

'Yes, dear. They had a little daughter,' Rebecca answered.

They halted a short distance away from the grieving couple and waited respectfully.

'What are we doing here, then?' Jack murmured.

'Luke wants to buy some things,' Rebecca replied.

The couple turned from the grave and moved leadenly towards them.

'Good day. I hear you're selling up,' Luke called.

'That is so,' replied the grieving father.

'We'd like to buy what you're not taking. We're just starting out ourselves.'

'I'll be glad to get rid of the cursed stuff.'

'Is that timber for sale? We need to build a kitchen.'

The man nodded dispiritedly.

'There's a full barrel of flour and a new oven you can have. We brought it up from Melbourne. I've hardly used it,' the sad-faced woman said.

The families tried to smile at each other as the afternoon breeze made the leaves mutter in the trees. Rebecca and Luke could not keep their eyes away from the little grave, thinking how appalled they would be if it was one of their own children lying in the hill.

'We wish you better luck than we've had at this godfor-saken place.'

'What was your little girl's name?' Lucy inquired.

'Lucy, ssshhh!' rebuked Rebecca.

The woman stooped down and put her hands on Lucy's shoulders. 'Her name was Molly. She was a little bit younger than you. She had golden hair – a bit longer than yours. I'm sure she would have liked to play with you.'

'But now she's up in heaven,' Lucy said.

'Yes, I'm sure she's with the angels,' the woman replied tearfully.

Everybody stood still. No one wished to be the first to quit this part of the wilderness which now would always be special. The breeze stirred the bunch of flowers on the grave. One rolled down the heaped clay. as the bellbirds called jubilantly to one another.

The Greenwoods retired early that night, exhausted from lugging home all their purchases. Luke had paid too much for the timber and the cast-iron stove, but nobody minded. Rebecca sat on Lucy's bed and read some more of *The Old Curiosity Shop*. Luke was at the table rubbing some of Doc's ointment into his hands. which were badly blistered from the shovel and cradle-handle.

'For she was dead. There upon her little bed, she lay at rest. The solemn stillness was no marvel now. She was dead. No sleep so beautiful and calm, so free from trace of pain, so fair to look upon. She seemed a creature fresh from the hand of God and waiting for the breath of life; not one who had lived and suffered death.' Rebecca raised her eyes from the book. Everybody remembered what had happened that day and little Nell's death reminded them of the grave on the hillside.

'It's very sad,' Lucy said.

'It's only a book,' Jack observed toughly.

'But it's just like that girl today. Mum, why does God let little girls die?' Lucy asked.

'He doesn't make them die,' Rebecca replied.

'But He could keep them alive, couldn't He?'

'It's not that simple, dear.'

'I don't think it's fair.'

'If we could see everything as God does, we would understand it probably is fair. It's part of a plan,' Luke said.

'What plan?' Clee demanded.

'Everything that happens to us is part of God's plan. We would understand if we could see it all,' Luke explained.

'So my father getting put in prison is part of the plan?'

'Y-e-e-s . . ,' Luke replied thoughtfully.

'And the little girl today?' Clee continued.

'She is with God and happier than she could ever be here,' Luke replied.

Clee turned this idea over in her mind, and clearly did not like it. 'I hope I'm not part of it – this plan,' she said flatly.

Jack reacted similarly. It was bad enough that ill-fortune had taken his father away and replaced him with one he didn't like, but for it to be part of a scheme – that would be adding insult to injury.

There was a furtive knock on the doorpost outside. Luke frowned as he rose. Who would be out on this freezing night? A wild and desperate-looking man stepped hurriedly in.

Luke's face clouded. 'Ned, I told you not to come here.' he whispered angrily.

'I had to, Luke. It's going to happen soon.'

64

Luke looked over the visitor's shoulder, apprehensive that he might have been followed. The man was very jumpy. Rebecca looked upset and frightened.

'My answer is still the same,' Luke said.

'Luke, listen to me. We need every man and gun we can get. There are troops on the way from Melbourne. We've got to stand and fight now. There may never be another chance.'

'Ned, I'm starting a new life here. I don't want any more trouble,' Luke whispered vehemently.

'But don't you see, we can do here what we couldn't do back home. We've got a chance to decide for ourselves,' the wild-eyed visitor pleaded.

Luke took Ned by the arm and steered him to the tent opening. 'Rebecca, I won't be long.'

Ned continued to urge Luke as they walked out of earshot. 'What's happened to you, Luke? When I told the others who you were, they all wanted you with us. Everybody knows of your work, back in England.'

Rebecca bit her lip in consternation as their voices grew faint in the distance.

'Who was that?' Jack asked. Rebecca did not answer, but stared sightlessly at the open book on her lap.

'Will Father be all right?' Lucy asked.

'Go to sleep now. Go on, it's late.'

'Who was it, though?' Jack persisted.

'Jack, be quiet, please. It was just an old friend of your father's. From England.' Rebecca's tone was unusually curt. The children wanted to know more, but they realized she was under a big strain. They laid their heads down to sleep, but their minds would not be still.

Jack was woken early the next morning, partly by the cold

which had penetrated his blankets. and partly by a whispered, but heated, exchange between Rebecca and Luke. They sat close together at the table so their talk would not wake the children.

'Luke. promise me you won't get mixed up in that thing at Eureka.'

'I've told you. I won't. I mean it.'

'Forbid him to come here again.'

'I can't do that. I won't have anything to do with the guns and the shooting, but he's a friend. I can't turn him away.'

'It's just that, with all that's happened, I couldn't stand anything more,' Rebecca pleaded, her voice cracking.

Luke stared lovingly at his wife. 'Becky. Becky, all that is behind me. It's no longer part of my life. You and Lucy and Jack are my life now.'

Jack's head seethed with a babble of thoughts. What was Luke doing, to make his mother so scared? Why did he hold her hand so tenderly if he was upsetting her? Jack was positive his real father wouldn't have upset his mother like this. But the love in Luke's voice when he spoke of Jack reached right across the room; and it confused the boy even more.

That morning, they were all up early, because the night had been so icy. Jack noticed that even the new purchases, the cast-iron oven, the huge barrel of flour, and other kitchen utensils could not banish Rebecca's frowns.

Everybody went outside to help build a new room on to their dwelling with the timber they had bought the day before. There had been a heavy frost. The tent was stiff with

66

it, and their hands were clumsy until the exercise thawed them. The youngsters worked with a will because they knew that the sooner they finished, the sooner they could get down to the river and make their tree-hut. Lin also lent a hand. He was expert at stripping sheets of bark from a special tree which, when overlapped and tied down, made an excellent roof.

'Can we go now?' Jack asked.

'I think so, children. You've put in a good morning's work.' Luke smiled. Rebecca sent them off with huge slices of bread and dripping which they munched happily as they walked down to meet Sean at the river.

Clee, as impetuous as ever, forged ahead. Although Jack would never have admitted it, his limp did slow him down. Clee rounded a bend in the track and ran slap-bang into Bojinda. He meant no harm, despite the spear and boomerang; but Clee got such a shock, she screamed at the top of her voice. Bojinda advanced, trying to calm her. This only added to Clee's fright, and she screamed again.

Lucy and Jack crashed through the undergrowth to her aid. Bojinda gave a last helpless gesture and melted like a shadow into the bush.

'What happened?' Jack gasped.

'It was . . . was . . . a black man.'

'Did he hurt you?' Lucy asked.

'I just got a fright,' she replied, shaking her head. 'I'm all right.'

They all gazed at the spot where the aborigine youth had disappeared.

Sean sat on the bank of the river under their tree, trimming saplings with a hatchet. A pile of rope was by his side. 'You look as though you've seen a ghost, he observed as they walked up.

'No, he was real all right,' Clee assured him.

'Who?'

'An aborigine. He had a spear and a...' She mimed the motion of throwing a boomerang.

'Boomerang,' Sean suggested.

She nodded.

'Do they hurt people?' asked Lucy.

'I don't know. Depends what you do to them, I suppose,' Sean replied.

'They said in Melbourne, sometimes they kill you,' Jack said.

'It used to happen,' Sean declared.

'Do they eat people?' Lucy inquired.

' 'Course not. Don't worry about it. Come on, we've got to get more logs for the hut.' Sean headed nonchalantly off into the bush.

'I think we should all stick together,' Lucy said tremulously.

'Good idea,' agreed Clee.

'Come on, Jack. You're not scared, are you?' Sean taunted.

'No,' Jack replied unconvincingly.

'Come on,' Sean chuckled.

They all set out to forage for saplings. Jack, Clee and Lucy looked over their shoulders constantly. But no terrible fate befell them as they laboured to construct their tree-hut. After gathering a large pile of saplings, they hauled them up to where the tree forked. By lashing them together, they constructed a platform. They then built the walls. Sean hacked scarves into the corner uprights to accept the side pieces. The girls were particularly good at tying knots. Jack did most of the climbing up and down.

Sean leaned over Clee, who was just fastening one log to another with twine. 'Hey, Clee, make sure they're real knots. Not like the ones your father ties you up with.'

'Who says they're not real knots?'

'Me!' said Sean.

Clee pulled a face.

They decided to take a rest. They settled back wearily on the uneven floor, admiring their achievement.

Jack laboured up the trunk with the last saplings. He was not too pleased to see his fellow-workers lolling around taking it easy. 'Hey, what's the big idea?'

'Just making sure everything's level, aren't we, girls?'

Jack had to grin.

The limb on which the tree-hut rested jutted over the river, so water was visible through the wide cracks in the floor.

'We could fish from here, too,' Lucy commented. Everybody nodded. They liked that idea.

Their self-congratulation was rudely interrupted by Ted's barking voice. 'Hey, you up there, better shove off if you know what's good for you.'

'We're happy where we are. It's a good place, isn't it?' Sean provoked him.

They all looked over the edge of the tree-hut at the angry young ruffian.

'Yeah, that's why I chose it. So scram.'

'Aren't you getting a sore neck, Ted?' Sean jeered.

'I'm coming back with some of my mates. You won't think it's so funny then.' Ted turned and retreated.

'Looks like war,' Sean remarked with mock-seriousness. 'And for that we need ammunition. Let's get ready.'

He and Jack waded into the river up to their thighs, reached down and pulled up thick, black river-mud. They dumped it on the bank and returned for more. The girls made large trays from strips of bark.

Sean picked up a lump of mud. 'Now watch closely,' he instructed. He rolled the mud between his hands to form a ball, then dropped it into the sand. He rolled it again. He placed the mud ball on to the bark trays. 'Got the idea?'

The others grinned and followed suit. After a couple of attempts, they were all expert mudball makers. When they had made a hundred or so, they carried them up to the tree-hut. They then lay back to wait for Ted and his army to return.

They didn't have to wait long. 'You've had it,' bawled Ted, to announce their arrival.

Jack peered over the wall of the tree-hut and saw Ted, Bobby and another two henchmen advancing.

Sean grinned evilly. 'That's the cleanest they're going to be all day.'

'You're outnumbered,' shouted Ted.

'What about us?' Clee shouted back.

'Girls don't count,' Bobby retorted scornfully.

'We'll see about that,' Lucy muttered.

'Do you give in?' Ted yelled.

'I can't hear you, Ted. You'll have to come closer,' Sean returned.

Ted moved forward. 'I said, do you surrender?'

Sean stood up quickly and let loose a mudball, catching

Ted right in the middle of his chest and splattering sludge everywhere.

Ted was almost speechless with rage. 'You ... you ... mongrels. Come on! Let's get them!' Ted, Bobby, and their lieutenants charged.

A fusillade of mudballs whistled down to greet them and they were halted by the withering fire. The defenders screamed with laughter and triumph. The projectiles were very effective – cold, wet, blinding and very unpleasant.

The attackers rallied and started scaling the tree, vowing vengeance. They tried to reach the limb on which the hut rested, but Sean and Jack engaged them in hand-to-hand combat. Lucy and Clee kept up the barrage of mudballs. Because the defenders had a surer footing, they were able to dislodge their attackers easily and they plummeted into the water below. They shrieked as they hit the icy river.

They scrambled up the bank, shaking their heads to clear them of water. 'You're dead now,' Ted squawked as he shinned up the tree. Once more, the defenders were able to repel them and they ended up taking another ducking. Thankfully, by now, all of them – even the drenched losers – were beginning to enjoy themselves. Up they came again. The mudballs ran out.

Now that their eyes were no longer full of grit, they were able to do battle on a more equal footing. Sean almost forced Bobby to fall backwards off the platform, when the attacker shifted his weight and wrenched Sean after him. The same fate befell Jack; Ted and he plunged into the water, locked together. All four youths regained the bank and continued the fight.

After a short wrestle, Sean sent Bobby packing. But Jack

was not so fortunate: Ted had got the better of him and was circling him, ready to finish him off. Jack's nose was bleeding and he was scared.

'Remember what Lin taught you,' Lucy shouted. Jack registered this as Ted made his move. Jack simply pivoted and blocked. Ted pawed the air. The others stood around watching the contest.

'You're scared, aren't you, Sharp?' Ted scoffed at Jack.

'No,' Jack gasped shakily.

'You are. You're a scaredy-cat, Sharp. A weakling and a cripple.'

'I'd be scared of someone as stupid as you, Ted,' Sean shouted.

Ted glared at Sean and made another charge. Jack repeated his skilful sidestep and, shaking his head like a goaded bull, Ted overran again. The spectators were by now enjoying this exhibition of guile on the part of Jack.

Ted grunted and charged again, his fists pumping. Jack swivelled, but this time to the other side. So great was Ted's momentum, that he pitched off the bank into the river. Everybody laughed, including his own men. Ted clambered up the bank, a defeated man.

Hiding in thick bush not ten paces away, Bojinda stared at these strange goings-on in utter bemusement.

Because they had got up so early, the day seemed to be lasting for ever. In fact, Jack had noticed that time seemed to pass differently out here in the wilderness. Back in Melbourne, where there were clock towers, church bells and school, the day had a fixed shape to it. Here, time was like a concertina; sometimes a day flashed past as though all the events were squeezed together, and sometimes it stretched out endlessly.

They decided to play hide-and-seek; any game with a lot of running in it would dry off their wet clothing. Lucy covered her eyes and started counting as the others sped off.

It didn't happen entirely by accident that Jack ended up sharing the same hiding-place as Clee. He had become very intrigued by the tough-minded young artiste. They both hid under a huge tree which had been blown down in a winter storm and now lay on its side, forming a canopy of leaves and branches. They burrowed deep into the foliage. They could just hear Lucy sing out, 'Ninety-nine ... one hundred. Coming, ready or not.' They sat with their backs against the old tree and relaxed.

'I've never really been into the bush like this before,' Clee said.

'I hadn't either till I came here,' said Jack. They grinned at each other.

'Jack, why was Ted calling you Sharp when you were fighting him?'

Jack did not answer straight away. He picked up a piece of bark and shredded it slowly as they talked. ' 'Cause that's my name.'

'Your name is Jack Greenwood.'

'No, it's not. My father's name was Sharp.'

'But ... But he died two years ago, didn't he?'

'Doesn't change anything.'

'Well ... I mean ... it seems funny that your mother and Lucy call themselves Greenwood and you don't.'

Jack suddenly ripped the bark into pieces and flung them

to the ground. Clee was taken aback at the violence of his feelings.

'He's a coward!' Jack exclaimed.

'A coward?'

'He doesn't stand up for himself.'

'What . . . ?' Clee didn't understand.

'Back in Melbourne and here, he lets people push him around. My real father never let anybody push him around.'

'But Luke is a good father. He's . . .' Clee cast around for the right word.

'He's weak.'

'He's gentle and . . .' Clee shook her head.

'Who cares about that! My father was a real good fighter. He could bash anybody up.'

'Who cares about that!' Clee said, mimicking Jack.

'You've got to bash people up who try to walk over you.' said Jack.

Clee clicked her tongue and tossed her head in disgust. The silly aggressiveness of men seemed to be getting an early start in the anger-filled boy. Jack knew, deep down, that what he had said wasn't quite true, but to abandon it meant he would have to start the painful trek away from his father towards Luke. A difficult silence fell between them, with both brooding on different things.

At last Clee exclaimed feelingly. 'At least you've got a father. And one who isn't in prison. And a mother!'

It was Jack's turn now to be surprised at her vehemence. She swallowed hard and turned her head away from Jack, so that he would not see how close she was to crying.

*

74

Lucy was getting sick and tired of searching. They've hidden too far away, she thought. Her frustration made her reckless. While trying to peer around an overhang on the river bank, she missed her footing and tumbled into the water. The river was quite shallow near the bank, but every so often big holes were scoured by the torrential rains. The height from which she fell drove her down deep. She came up gasping and churning the water uselessly with her hands.

'Help! Help! Jack!' She arched her back, trying to keep her head above water, but it was no good. Down she went again. She fought to keep her mouth shut against the eager water. Up she came again, but she knew it was for the last time. The bright blue sky started to spin as her air gave out. The muddy waters swirled over her head and into her mouth as she slipped down into the murky depths.

Her fading senses were restored by a sudden sharp pain in her scalp. Her hair felt as though it was being pulled out by the roots. She was drawn up . . . to stare straight into the face of Bojinda. He muttered something in a language she didn't understand and, holding her head out of the water, he struck out for the shore. Arriving, he waded out with her in his arms. Lucy's white dress and pallid face contrasted sharply with his black body, glossy with river water.

He laid her on the grass, where she gasped and spluttered.

'Safe now. Safe now. Good,' he said.

'Thank . . . you . . .' Lucy managed.

Sean, Jack and Clee broke cover at the same time and saw the aborigine leaning over the prostrate Lucy.

'Leave her alone,' Jack screamed.

Jack and Sean converged on Bojinda. It was quite plain

that the youngsters meant to attack him. In one swift motion he rose and made for the trees. So agile was he, and so at home in the bush, that he vanished before the boys could even think of following.

They ran to Lucy's side.

'What did he do to you?' Jack demanded.

'Did he hurt you?' Sean asked.

'I fell into the river . . .'

'Did he push you in?' Jack asked.

'No, I slipped.'

'Were you trying to get away?' Sean asked.

Lucy had become exasperated by their misunderstanding, but she was still breathless from her ordeal, so Clee had to silence the boys. 'Shut up you two. Let her talk.'

Lucy glanced gratefully at Clee. 'He was trying to save me. I almost drowned and he rescued me.'

Jack and Sean looked abashed. They nodded.

Clee turned to Jack. 'What a pity he got away. Now you can't bash him up. You must be very disappointed,' she said, sarcastically.

Jack dropped his eyes. That shot had found its mark.

When Lucy had recovered, they set out for home. The sunset was quite breathtaking. The huge brazen orb dipped below the horizon, trailing avenues of blood and gold behind it. Their crowded day was beginning to tell on them as they plodded on.

Jack was bringing up the rear and when Lucy turned around to call to him, she glimpsed Bojinda.

'You boys stay here. I'll go back and talk to him. Come on, Clee.'

'Will you be all right?' Jack asked.

'If he'd wanted to do anything to harm me, he'd have done it by now, wouldn't he?'

The girls approached Bojinda cautiously. They came near and stopped. He stared back at them impassively.

'Thank you for helping me. My name is Lucy. Her name is Cleopatre. Clee.'

Bojinda regarded them a moment longer, then his face split into a smile, baring the whitest teeth they'd ever seen.

'I am Bojinda,' he said slowly with a funny intonation.

Lucy and Clee grinned also.

Lucy pointed at Sean and Jack some distance off. 'They are our friends. They mean no harm.'

Bojinda nodded. Clee waved the boys over. They arrived, looking a bit sheepish. They introduced themselves and shook hands. Bojinda did so clumsily, not sure of the formality, but he surprised them all by saying in good, but heavily accented English, 'I am pleased to meet you.'

'You speak good English.'

'Where did you learn?' Clee asked.

'I help a missionary go about...' He pointed far into the distance.

They had exhausted their stock of conversation and so made do with more nods and smiles. Bojinda suddenly said goodbye and walked away. For an instant, before he disappeared over a hill, he was caught against the copper sky, a silhouette of litheness and grace.

It seemed that the day, already crammed with surprises, had not quite finished with them. It was almost dark when they arrived home but, as they neared their encampment, they saw a sign nailed to a post outside. It read, 'Fresh-baked Bread. Threepence A Loaf.'

Rebecca was in a bubbly mood. She explained that the new oven was so efficient that she could bake ten loaves at once, and she had decided to sell off the extra. She had already sold thirty loaves that day; but the most satisfactory result of her new business was that Mr Lovejoy had stormed up purple with rage, and demanded that she stop. He wouldn't be able to sell his flour at such a profit with her undercutting him.

'And what did you say, Mum?' Lucy asked.

'I said, "Hard luck, Mr Lovejoy, hard luck".' She repeated the phrase triumphantly, to the acclaim of her children.

What a day of victories, mused Jack, as he fell asleep, his mind full of visions of Ted standing shocked and defeated in the river.

CHAPTER FIVE

Jack sat bolt upright and blinked as he tried to focus on what had woken him. Dawn light, glimmering on the canvas, had not yet made any impression on the lamp-light, so it was very early. Yet there was Doc Slope with his parents, grouped around the kitchen table. And there was that awful sound again. It was a gasping, agonized groan. Jack could now make out a fourth figure – it was Ned, the man who had come to see Luke some nights ago. His shirt was covered in blood and torn back to expose his shoulder.

Doc put down a surgical instrument and held up something small in his fingers. 'Well, Ned, I got it out, so you should heal up hunky-dory.'

The man called Ned nodded. He turned to Luke and muttered deliriously, 'We held on as long as we could ... didn't have enough guns. They overran us too quickly ... over a hundred mounted troopers ... butchered us.' Ned's voice caught and faltered with the memory.

Doc began to bind his arm with bandages. 'It's all right. Ned. Settle down, boy. Settle down.'

'All over. Dead. And we were so close.' Ned fell back in the chair, sweating and shaking.

'We'll have to put him in Marcel's caravan, out the back,' Luke whispered.

By now the girls were awake, too, and they exchanged astounded looks with Jack. Doc and Luke supported Ned out through the door.

Rebecca noticed that the children were awake. She came over with a solemn face and sat down on a bed.

'What's that man doing here again?' asked Jack.

'He is a friend of your father's. There's been some trouble over at the Eureka diggings.'

'What sort of trouble?'

'I'm not sure, Jack – between the government soldiers and some of the diggers. Some of the men didn't want to continue paying for their licences. So they refused and the troops tried to make them.'

'What was wrong with him?' Clee asked.

'He had a bullet in his shoulder,' Rebecca replied.

The children thought about this for a while. 'Did that man ask Luke to join in with them?' Jack asked. Rebecca nodded. 'Why didn't he?'

'Because I told him not to.'

'Because he's scared!' Jack declared.

'Shut up, Jack,' Clee said shortly.

'I wish I'd been there. I can use a gun. I would have joined in,' Jack said.

'And got yourself killed, you silly boy.'

For Jack, this was yet more evidence of Luke's cowardice. When the men returned he could scarcely restrain himself from accusing Luke.

Rebecca rose quickly and spoke to him in an urgent whisper. 'Luke, can't he stay somewhere else?'

'He shouldn't be moved. Anyway, Doc's a known sympathizer. His is the first place they'll search.' Luke replied.

'Danks suspects you, too.'

'Becky, it's going to be all right. He'll move on in a couple of days. Don't worry.'

Rebecca was very unhappy. But she knew Luke's mind was made up, and anyway, she did not really want to turn a sick man out. 'You never quite leave your past behind, do you?' she mused.

'We can't. It's what we are,' Luke said. Rebecca nodded. 'Now don't worry. I'll tell you what, Becky, children, we'll give ourselves a holiday,' Luke said brightly.

The children were absolutely delighted to hear this. While Rebecca prepared some food for a picnic, they got their chores over and done with so they could make an early start.

Lovejoy was extremely edgy. He didn't like the bandits coming to his store. He hopped from one stilt-like leg to the other. 'Are you sure nobody saw you arrive?'

'You know us, Uriah, invisible as the wind,' Ernest replied. 'Isn't that right, Bones?'

But Bones was not quite sure what he meant, and frowned as he puzzled over it.

'I've got a job for you,' Lovejoy said.

'Let's talk about the payment first, Uriah.'

'Don't you think about anything but money?'

'Like jewellery, you mean?' Ernest commented cheekily.

Lovejoy narrowed his eyes menacingly. 'I've got some unwelcome competition. A woman has started baking bread and my sales of flour have dropped to almost nothing.'

'It's that kid's mother, isn't it?'

'How did you know?' Lovejoy inquired.

'Bones here went and bought some bread. Almost got himself seen by the kid, too.'

'It was real nice bread,' Bones remarked sunnily.

Lovejoy shot him a filthy look. 'I want them to suffer a little setback. Especially in the bread-making area.'

'I'll make them suffer all right.' Ernest hissed.

'Just a warning . . . so they realize how foolish it is to cross Uriah Lovejoy. Especially after I've been so good to them.'

Ernest and Bones easily gained entry to the Greenwood house, by pushing hard on the flimsy door. Ernest had been thrown out of his home when he was twelve for stealing his father's wages, so he'd never had much home life. The sight of the neat and cosy family-dwelling annoyed him in a way he could not understand. He wrenched the 'BLESS THIS HOUSE' plaque off the centre-post and hurled it to the ground. He then pulled the heavy barrel of flour over and ground it into the dirt floor.

'Come on, Bones, get on with it.'

Bones half-heartedly messed up the beds. The tent-and-timber addition looked really nice to him, just the sort of place he'd like to live in himself.

Ernest heaved on the still half-hot cast-iron stove. He finally dislodged it and tipped it forward on to the hearth stones. There was a loud crack as it fractured. Ernest was about to spread the embers along the wooden walls when Bones clamped a hand on to his shoulder.

'Ernie, we don't have to burn the place down, do we?'

'What's the matter with you, Bones? Getting soft?' But

Bones' hand remained where it was and his eyes were unswerving. 'All right, you idiot.'

Ernest swept all the crockery and jars of foodstuffs off the sideboard, then stamped them to splinters. Then with one last destructive gesture, he slashed a long cut in the tent with his shiny knife.

The noise of the destruction carried as far as the caravan and broke into Ned's delirious sleep. He was able to lever himself up to peer out of the small window and saw what the two intruders were up to. He stumbled to the door and, with his last strength, shouted at them. But Ernest just turned and laughed at him. Ned collapsed back on the bed, with pain stabbing through his shoulder.

Some distance from Jericho there was a wide, sweeping bend where the river had dumped silt for thousands of years. On this rich soil, lush green grass had grown. It was flat, clear of scrub, and perfect for cricket. Jack, Sean, Clee and Lucy were setting up the wickets. Jack hammered in the trimmed, sharpened sticks with their home-made bat. They had decided to take Sean into their confidence over the fugitive.

'What'll they do to that man ... Ned ... if they find him?' Clee wondered.

'Hang him, probably,' Sean answered baldly.

'We wouldn't let them!' Jack declared.

'How'd we stop them?' Lucy asked.

'We'd stop them all right,' Sean said.

'Yes, we'd stop them,' Jack agreed, hammering the last wicket in viciously.

'What does the government ever do for us? They just sit

in Melbourne, counting our money and sending it back to England,' Sean proclaimed angrily.

'Sean's right. We don't need Danks.' Jack took up the cry.

Down by the river Lin was lighting a fire while Rebecca unpacked the picnic food. Luke dumped a pile of driftwood on to the fire.

'It's a beautiful country, don't you think, Lin?' Luke said.

'Ah yes. I have never seen the sun so bright as here.'

'And it's been very kind to us, too. Do you know, I sold eighty loaves this week?' Rebecca said.

'I just wish I could find some more gold. Maybe *I* should play the games and let Lucy dig for it,' Luke commented ruefully.

'We can't complain about our luck ... not really, Luke,' Rebecca chided him.

'Why do you say "luck"? You are worthy of reward because of goodness,' Lin said.

Luke and Rebecca didn't understand what he meant. They looked at him quizzically.

'Those poor people you bought things from ... you paid too much. You think heaven is blind? It sees and helps you.' The old Chinaman was in closer contact with his spiritual world than were the Westerners.

Jack shouted from the cricket pitch: 'Come on. We need to pick teams!'

He explained to Lin the rules of cricket. 'You must hit the ball and then run between the wickets. Those things over there.'

'And what is this game called?' Lin asked.

'Cricket. Cricket,' Jack repeated, so Lin could remember the word.

'Ah, cricket-cricket.'

'No, just one. Cricket.'

'Ah, cricket. We do not have in China.'

'Here, Lin, you bat first,' Jack offered.

Lin was not too keen, but everybody cheered him on. He took up the batting stance with some hesitation. Jack picked up the old battered ball and ran back to bowl. Despite his limp, Jack was a good fast-bowler. He steamed in and slammed in a fast one.

Lin's reactions were lightning-quick . . . he hooked it for a six. Jack adopted the time-honoured stance of a fast-bowler who has been punished. He stared at Lin with a mixture of reproach and disbelief. Everybody else clapped and whistled.

'Are you sure you don't play it in China?' Jack asked.

At the edge of the clearing, Bojinda stood watching. It looked like the oddest tribal dance he'd ever seen. Plucking up courage, he ventured out from his cover and walked towards them.

Lucy was the first to see him. She rushed over. 'Bojinda. Bojinda. Hello.'

Bojinda smiled. The others ran up and exchanged greetings.

Lucy led Bojinda over to her parents. 'Mum and Dad, this is the boy we were telling you about. Bojinda.' Luke, Rebecca and Bojinda smiled and bobbed in greeting. Lin bowed very deeply.

'Where does your family live?' Luke inquired.

Bojinda pointed over the faraway hills, but did not elaborate.

'Do you want to play cricket?' Jack asked.

'Is it a . . . dance?'

Everybody smiled. 'This is a game – cricket,' Jack explained.

'Like a corroboree?' Bojinda asked.

Jack did not know what he meant. Lin knew quite a few aboriginal words and explained that a corroboree was a tribal meeting.

'You have turn,' said Lin, giving the bat to Jack. 'Poor old bones must sit down.'

'Here comes Doc,' Sean exclaimed, pointing. Doc was some distance away, labouring under the weight of his cumbersome camera.

'He's got that funny box thing with him,' Clee observed.

'Come on. Let's play on,' Jack cried.

Looking like a champion, Jack turned to face Sean. Sean bowled a slow spinner. Jack read the ball, advanced on it and clubbed it very hard. Bojinda was able to snatch from the air a boomerang returning faster than the eye could see, so it was an easy matter for him to stick his hand up and catch the ball.

'Howzat! everybody screamed.

Bojinda looked a bit embarrassed at his success. Jack looked wholly furious. He was very reluctant to move. 'Sorry,' Bojinda called.

'Don't be sorry. It was great. Walk, Jack. Fair's fair,' they all shouted. Jack shook his head and left the pitch.

After lunch, Doc offered to take a photograph of them all. Looking apprehensively at the odd contraption, they formed up into a compact group.

'Does it hurt?' Clee wanted to know.

'Is it magic?' asked Jack.

'No, this is science. This is no hocus-pocus or mumbo-jumbo,' Doc explained. 'Now you must smile and keep very still for as long as you can.'

'Can we scratch ourselves?'

'Have a good scratch now if you must, Sean.'

All the youngsters started to scratch like chimpanzees. Bojinda gazed at the odd-looking contrivance as if staring into the mouth of a cannon. Eventually they all settled down and Doc took the photograph.

Tired and happy from their long hike, the cricketers trooped up the main street. Jack had recovered his good humour because he had scored an unbeaten fifty in the second innings. They were all rather surprised to see Mr Lovejoy standing on the verandah of his store, taking in the evening air. Next to him on the railing perched Jasper. Lovejoy favoured them all with a smile false enough to curdle milk.

'What a lovely day it's been, hasn't it.'

They were all taken aback by his pleasantness.

'Yes, it has, Mr Lovejoy. Good evening to you,' Luke greeted him.

'What's he so happy about?' Jack said to Sean.

'Must have diddled some old lady out of sixpence.' But Jack was about to have his question answered in a most disturbing way. Rebecca was the first to see their vandalized dwelling, her precious oven cracked and useless, her flour spoiled, her kitchen wrecked. Luke walked around, speechless, righting the furniture. Lucy took one look and burst into tears. Clee gazed at the destruction, dismay giving way to anger. Jack ran over to where the plaque lay twisted and broken on the ground.

Luke remembered Ned and ran out. Ned lay in the caravan sweating with fever and ashen from loss of blood.

'Ned, are you all right?'

'I ... couldn't ... do anything.'

Sean and Jack entered.

'Who was it?' Luke asked.

'Two men. Never seen them before.'

'Was one big and one really skinny?' Jack prompted.

'That's right.'

'It must have been the bushrangers!' Jack shouted.

'Bet it was Lovejoy who put them up to it,' Sean added.

'Let's get him,' Jack cried.

'Just a minute, Jack, we don't know for certain that he had anything to do with it,' Luke interrupted.

' 'Course we do.'

'We can't take the law into our own hands because ...'

'Because you're scared, that's why.'

'Jack, I won't have you ...'

But Jack spun on his heel and clattered out in disgust. Sean was embarrassed by Jack's insolence and smiled apologetically, then he too left. Luke wiped the wet brow of the injured man but his thoughts were on the unhealing injury between him and Jack which, although not bloody, caused just as much pain.

Doc Slope was never happier than when his door was tightly closed for the night and he was at home with his bottles, jars, boxes and crocks full of powders, mixtures, tinctures and salts. He sat at a table with all the bits and pieces of the new science of photography spread around him. At his right hand was his familiar bottle of sourmash whiskey. The flickering of the lamp filled the room with huge pulsing silhouettes. There was a knock at the door. Doc scowled until he saw who his visitors were.

'We've come to ask you for help,' Jack began.

'And you could not have picked a man more ready to give it, my boy.'

'You see, Lovejoy has broken in and wrecked our tent and smashed the stuff Mother bakes bread with . . .'

'Why, that low-bred varmint!'

'And we want to make sure he doesn't try anything like that again,' Jack said darkly, 'but we don't know how to stop him.'

Doc tossed back another drink and stared at the boys thoughtfully. 'I've got one piece of advice for you boys. Softly, softly. Do you follow me?' He put his forefinger to his lips. The boys nodded, trying to work out what he meant. 'There's more ways than one to skin a cat. Do you follow me?' The boys nodded again, but exchanged a hasty look of puzzlement.

Doc went to a cluttered shelf and got down a large jar full of blue crystals. He solemnly deposited this in front of the boys. Then he stooped and hefted up a box full of white powder and set this next to the jar.

'Use your God-given intelligence to lay your enemy low. Not brute force. Not violence, but science. Do you follow me?'

The boys were absolutely in his spell now and nodded gravely, although they still weren't sure what he was getting at.

'What have we here? Mmmm?' Doc asked.

'Not sure,' Sean admitted.

'Don't know either.'

'Then I, Doc Cassius Slope, will tell you. You have here plaster of Paris for setting bones, and potassium permanganate for disinfecting and cleansing. And what have these things to do with teaching the repellent Mr Lovejoy a lesson he won't forget? Come closer and I will tell you.'

Jack and Sean shuffled closer as Doc leaned forward.

The boys had no trouble finding their way down the uneven street because a huge harvest moon rode high in the sky, plating the ugly shanty town with silver. Jack carried a small sack and Sean's pockets bulged. Giggling nervously, they arrived at the back entrance of Lovejoy's shop and searched it for a way in. There was a fanlight above the door which was half open. Sean leaned forward and Jack climbed up on his shoulders. He tried to force the fanlight but the opening was too small to admit him.

'How are we going to get in?' whispered Jack.

'Use a brick.'

'Hey, bet you Clee could get through here.'

Now that Rebecca and Luke had their own room in the new timber annex, Lucy and Clee talked for hours before going to sleep. Sometimes Jack was forced to throw his boots across the room to shut them up.

'You know what your father was saying ... that everything's part of God's plan,' Clee mused. Lucy nodded her head dully – she was still quite upset. 'I wonder where this fits in. I mean, this place being wrecked.'

Lucy heaved a big sigh. She spoke slowly. 'Well, God must have a reason. Otherwise it's not fair. I mean that the bad men are allowed to harm Mother and Father ... who are good.'

'I don't think it's fair that my father gets dragged off and put in prison either.'

'You've just got to accept it. Not accepting things is what's wrong with Jack.'

Clee turned and faced Lucy realizing that behind her young eyes worked a wise mind.

'I'm sure it'll be all right in the end. Father says everything always turns out,' Lucy added seriously.

Suddenly Jack slithered underneath the edge of the tent. 'Hey, Clee, can you come and give us a hand?'

Lovejoy was so frightened of being seen with his hired rogues that he lit no lamp in his store when they visited him at night. 'A guinea, as agreed. Now go.' Ernest and Bones had spent the day in one of the illicit grog-tents. 'Go! Go! Go!' Lovejoy hissed at the glassy-eyed bandits.

'All in good time, Uriah. We've got a little bit of information that might tickle you,' Ernest slurred. 'You don't seem to like this fellow Greenwood, is that right?'

'Perhaps . . .' Lovejoy was intrigued.

'Well, I reckon he's looking after one of the rebels who got wounded at Eureka. We saw him in a caravan out the back.'

'So our Mr Greenwood has slipped back into his old ways, has he?' said Lovejoy, rubbing his hands. 'I'm sure Mr Danks will be most interested in this piece of information.'

Clee and Jack returned to where Sean was hiding behind the wood-pile. Sean had heard a noise from the store and told them to be quiet. The youngsters were startled to see Lovejoy push the bushrangers out. They were also surprised to see Jasper perched comfortably on his shoulder.

'Keep your voices down, you fools. I don't want anybody to notice you.'

'Is that any way to treat friends. Uriah,' Ernest sniggered.

The bushrangers stumbled off into the night, bumping into each other.

'We'll pay a visit to officer Danks, then we'll go and catch you some big juicy mice. Just the night for it. What a beautiful moon! A much nicer planet than the sun, wouldn't you say?' Jasper's eyes seemed to glow uncannily bright.

The youngsters looked at each other, aghast. 'Come on! We haven't got long,' Jack said when Lovejoy was out of sight.

The boys lifted Clee up. She had no trouble in wriggling her supple body through the small window. She dropped to the floor and opened the door for the boys.

Once inside, they padded down the passage into the shop. Jack headed for the flour barrels. He lifted the lids and poured in the contents of the small sack.

'What is it?' Clee asked.

'Plaster of Paris.'

'What does it do?' Clee asked.

'You'll see.' Sean found the milk pails and tipped in the contents of his pockets.

'I'd love to be able to see it.'

'What did you put in?'

'Potassium perm ... perm ... or something.' Sean stumbled over the unfamiliar words and Clee was none the wiser.

They said goodnight to Sean and headed for home. Jack was walking on air. He had longed to get back at Lovejoy, now he had. His delight was short-lived, however.

Danks stood at the door, browbeating Luke. The youngsters glided as near as they could to hear what was going on.

'If what you say is true, you will have no objection to me looking around, will you?' hectored Danks.

'It's very late. Can't you come back in the morning?'

'You must take me for a fool, Mr Greenwood. Your radical views are well known.'

'He's come to search for Ned,' Jack whispered.

Jack and Clee melted back into the night. They opened the caravan door as noiselessly as they could. Ned lay on the bed, looking more comfortable. He turned as the children entered.

'Ned, the police have come to search. You'll have to get out of here.'

Ned made a feeble attempt to rise, and Clee and Jack tried to help him. Footsteps and muffled voices approached. The youngsters looked around in panic.

Clee had a brainwave: she threw open the magic chest, and she and Jack helped Ned to get in. Clee was just closing the lid when Luke and Danks arrived outside the door.

'It's not even my property. I can't really let you in,' Luke stalled.

'Fiddlesticks, Mr Greenwood. Out of my way immediately.'

On the spur of the moment, Clee snatched up a false beard and wig and put them on. She jumped into bed and pulled the covers up to her chin. In the dim light, she could have been taken for a man.

The men entered. They were both startled to see Jack standing there sheepishly.

'Nobody in here, eh! You have a lot of trouble telling the truth, don't you?'

Before Luke could ask Jack what he was doing there, Danks saw the figure in the bed. He unholstered his pistol and tensed; he was in the presence of a dangerous fanatic.

'And who is that?'

'Umm ... It's Cleopatre,' Jack answered.

'Oh it is, eh? She's grown a beard now, has she? All right, on your feet slowly, Mister. You realize what the penalty for harbouring fugitives from the law is, Mr Greenwood?'

Clee turned around and stood up. Danks blinked, gaped and his mouth dropped open in confusion. The beard and wig were pulled off to reveal an impishly grinning girl.

'I told you it was Clee,' Jack smiled. Even Luke grinned, though mainly with relief.

Danks gritted his teeth. 'I'm going to turn this place upside down.' He surveyed the caravan and his eyes lighted on the magic chest. 'What's in there?'

'Nothing,' Clee lied.

'Open it!'

'My father's got the key with him.'

'Then I'll have to break it open.'

Clee suddenly dropped into a sideshow barker's tone. 'No, Sir. It's one of our main attractions and I can prove positively to you that there is absolutely nobody in there. Watch!' She extracted the swords from their rack and slashed them through the air so that they whistled viciously. Danks shrank back, a look of abject terror on his face. His gun wavered and dropped.

'Sharp as a razor,' Clee said. She rammed the swords into their slots till they stuck out the other side. Jack hoped that she knew how to do the trick.

'If there was anybody in there, Mr Danks, his blood would be gushing out by now. No living creature could still be alive.'

Danks swallowed hard. Things were moving a bit too fast for him. Jack looked green. He had seen a live man go in there; he hoped he would step out the same way.

Danks had had enough. He had completely lost the initiative and stood there, entirely at a loss. 'He may have slipped through my fingers this time but don't forget, Mr Greenwood, I've got my eye on you. You may have got away with it on this occasion, but don't try it again.' He glared threateningly at Jack as well. 'I've got more important things to do than waste my time with children.'

He turned on his heel, but spoilt his exit by bumping into some masks hanging from the roof, and tripped down the steps.

Jack and Clee waited for a moment, then Clee went to the chest and opened it. Luke helped Ned out, shaken but not hurt. Jack and Clee started to laugh, and soon the men joined in as well.

Lovejoy wrapped up a slab of cheese for an old woman.

'That's one shilling, please.'

'One shilling. But last week it was only tenpence.'

Jack and Sean entered the shop trying to look casual. Lovejoy and Jasper watched them suspiciously, sensing something odd in their expressions.

'That was Australian cheese and this is English. A vastly superior product, you have to admit,' he said, dismissing the old lady. He turned to the boys, his instincts alert at their air of studied innocence. 'What do you two want?'

'Nothing at the moment, Mr Lovejoy,' Sean answered sweetly. 'May we just look around for a minute?' Before Lovejoy could throw them out, a digger entered with a large glass jar.

'Fill it with milk.'

'Yes, Sir.' The boys craned forward to see what effect their sabotage had had. They couldn't have been more pleased; the milk which Lovejoy ladled into the digger's jar was purple. Another miner entered with a pail. Both he and the first customer goggled uncomprehendingly. Lovejoy followed their eyes and dropped the ladle with a yelp.

'What ... I don't ...'

'That cow is sick,' the digger observed. Lovejoy swiftly opened the other pail. He fetched up a ladleful. It was an even deeper purple.

'Look ... I'm very sorry ...

'Give us our money back.'

'Reckon I'll drink water today.' The diggers gave Lovejoy a dirty look and clumped out.

Lovejoy noticed the two boys grinning fit to split their faces. 'And what are you smiling about?'

'Who? Us?'

'Are we smiling?' Jack asked.

Lovejoy began to mottle with rage.

'As a matter of fact, Mr Lovejoy, we might be able to help you out.'

'Help me?'

'We know a way of stopping milk from turning purple.'

'You little scoundrels!' Jasper gave a low screech of contempt. Before Lovejoy could take the matter further, an old prospector hobbled in. He carried a piece of baked damper, a sort of rough scone eaten on the goldfields. He was very angry.

'Lovejoy, are you happy with the flour you're selling at the moment?'

'Happy? Why, yes.'

'Well, I'm not.' He dropped the damper on the floor with a crash. It was as hard as rock.

Lovejoy's eyes were drawn up from where it had landed by the entrance of a strapping young Irishman. He walked wordlessly to the counter and deposited a slab of damper on it with a clunk. He reached over to a rack of hammers and chipped a piece off, then proffered it ominously to Lovejoy.

'If you don't give me my money back. I'm going to make you eat this,' the huge Irishman said.

Amongst all the qualities that went to make up Lovejoy's character, none was so highly developed as his sense of personal safety. He grabbed a handful of silver from the till and thrust it at the old timer and the Irishman.

They marched out again, the young man grumbling, 'You're lucky I didn't break your head open with it, by St Patrick you are.'

By now Sean and Jack were doubled up with laughter. 'Quite a bit of bad luck this morning, Mr Lovejoy,' commented Sean.

'As I was saying, there is a way that you can stop your milk turning purple and your flour turning to stone,' Jack offered innocently.

'And how do I do that?' hissed Lovejoy like an angry snake.

'Simple. You just leave my family alone.'

It seemed as if there was some sort of volcanic activity going on inside the shopkeeper's head. A vein started to throb on his temple and his face was turning crimson.

Finally he erupted. 'You little monsters.' He launched himself at them. Jasper followed his master's lead and swooped on the boys, flapping and screeching.

Jack and Sean jumped out of their way and headed for the door. Just as it seemed Lovejoy would pinion Jack with his outstretched hands, Sean pulled over a barrel of shovels and brooms; Lovejoy tripped on them and went sprawling. The boys burst out into the sunlight, leaving their pursuer spread-eagled on the floor, looking like a crashed praying mantis. Jasper alighted on his head and looked sympathetically down on him.

The next night Rebecca prepared a baked rabbit, surrounded by lots of Lin's vegetables. The occasion was the departure of Ned. Doc had visited him earlier and declared that the infection had gone and that he was fit enough to move on to another place of refuge. Rebecca was in very good spirits because they would no longer be liable to charges of harbouring a criminal. Luke was delighted to see her natural happiness return.

Ned wore one of Luke's shirts; his own had had to be burnt because of the bloodstains. 'Thank you all for looking after me. Especially Clee for saving my skin,' Ned grinned.

'It was your skin I was most worried about,' Luke joked.

'And thank you, Luke and Rebecca. I know how much you've risked by looking after me.' He turned to Jack and Lucy. 'You should be very proud of your parents. They are very brave people. Your father is still remembered in Dudley for what he . . .'

Luke cleared his throat, interrupting Ned. 'All that was long ago. It's probably best left in the past, Ned.'

'Many's the worker who still blesses your name, Luke,' Ned said.

Jack looked at Luke, perplexed. But before he could ask any questions, Luke changed the subject.

'By the way, Jack, we had a rather curious visit from Mr Lovejoy today.' Jack dropped his eyes, dreading what was coming. 'Your mother and I don't know what to make of it.' Clee and Lucy looked apprehensively at Jack, also waiting for the worst. Luke went on, 'He asked me to tell you that there will be no more vandalism against us from now on. Rebecca and I don't know what he means by it or why he should want to tell you. Do you know anything about it?'

The children could hardly suppress smiles of relief.

'Um . . . no, not really . . .' Jack said hollowly.

'Nothing at all?' Rebecca inquired sternly.

Jack shook his head in an unconvincing rendition of innocence. Luke's severe expression softened and he smiled at Jack. Jack couldn't hold back his mirth any longer, and he smiled in return. They seemed ready to accept each other's different way of doing things for once. A small chink had been chipped in the wall which separated them.

Although it gave Jack a good feeling to smile at his stepfather, that night, before he went to sleep, he apologized to his real father for the small betrayal. So the chink was closed up once more but, thankfully. no wall, once breached, even a little, is ever as strong again.

CHAPTER
SIX

There was a real whiff of spring in the air. New growth, bright lime-green, glowed on the trees. A fuzz of grass appeared where the waterlogged ground was slowly draining. The birds had started their seasonal squabbling and parading and fooling around. The cruel iron chill of winter was giving way to the squally mellowness of spring.

The youngsters had decided to build a raft to explore the river. Bojinda sat on the bank with them, lashing logs together. Sean had borrowed a hammer and some nails and was driving them in to make the craft sturdier. Lucy and Bojinda worked side by side. Perhaps because of their dramatic introduction, they had become firm friends.

'Why does your tribe keep away from Jericho, Bojinda?' Lucy asked.

'Many of my people got sick ... and some died ... The clayface not good for my people.'

Lucy held a knot in place while Bojinda tightened it, black and white hands pulling at the same rope together.

'But we get on all right,' Jack said.

Bojinda tied another knot, then he smiled sadly. 'Now we do.'

This seemed to sound a sour note. The others stared at

him, remembering the nasty things they'd heard the diggers say about the blacks. One man had boasted how he'd shot two of them at a remote diggings because he suspected them of theft.

Sean threw his hammer down, determined to dispel the gloom. 'It's ready. Let's launch it!'

With much heaving and shoving, they slid the raft into the water. After a few bobs, it stabilized and really looked the part.

Clee and Jack were allotted the first stint with the poles. They pushed out into the middle and allowed the sluggish current to tug them along. A great contentment settled on them as they drifted beneath the overhanging river gum-trees.

'Have you ever been across those hills, Bojinda?' Lucy wanted to know.

Bojinda looked in the direction of her pointing finger. 'A great spirit-lizard sleeps there and must not be woken.'

'Who makes up all your stories?' Jack asked.

'Not made up. But happened . . . in the dreaming.'

'Do you believe them?' Clee asked.

'I don't believe; I know,' Bojinda answered simply.

'Seems pretty funny to talk about the land and everything as though it's . . . alive,' Jack said.

'It is alive. Like us. Our mother and our father.'

The others thought about this and stared at their surroundings with new eyes. Jack knew that back in Melbourne he would have ridiculed such a silly idea; but out here, where the land was so big and man so small, he didn't feel like laughing at all. At that moment a kookaburra laughed its lunatic laugh, and Jack had the uncomfortable feeling it was scoffing at them.

Living on the goldfields was very expensive: a pound of potatoes could sometimes cost two shillings; and Lovejoy's mark-up on everything from boot-laces to candles was shocking. Rebecca and Luke had decided to order a new oven and more flour from a travelling merchant. The merchant had insisted on payment before he left, so many times had he been let down by the unreliable gold-rush population. Unfortunately he had not returned as promised. The consequence was that they had used up all their money.

'I'm useless, Becky. I've found absolutely nothing in months.'

'It's all luck, Luke. It's not your fault.'

'Everybody else has had a strike. Why not me?'

Rebecca crossed the kitchen and stood behind him with her hands on his shoulders. 'Stop blaming yourself.'

'I've got to face it. I haven't got the thirty shillings for this month's miner's licence.'

'We'll have to get one,' Rebecca said.

'But all our money's gone.'

Rebecca sighed in resignation. She'd already worked out what they had to do. 'Then we'll have to sell Lovejoy our rings.'

'No, Rebecca. We can't do that.'

'I don't doubt your love for me and you don't doubt my love for you, so we don't need jewellery to prove it.'

Luke nodded his head slowly. Suddenly, finding gold didn't seem all that important with riches like Rebecca so close.

With this agreed on, they trudged reluctantly up to the store and entered.

In an instant Lovejoy had a jeweller's glass screwed into his eye and was inspecting Rebecca's ring. He was positively drooling over it. Luke's ring was also on the counter.

'But we do not want to sell our rings, we want to pawn them . . . if that's the expression,' Rebecca said.

Lovejoy drew himself up to his full height and gazed down his nose at the penniless couple.

'I am not a pawnbroker. I am a merchant and trader in precious stones and metals.'

'In that case we're wasting your time.' Rebecca retrieved the rings from the counter and made to turn.

'Just a moment, Mrs Greenwood. Not so hasty. Please explain your proposal.'

'You will give us thirty pounds now and, unless we pay you back within the month, the rings are yours.'

'With the addition of some interest, of course. To redeem the rings you will have to pay me thirty-three pounds, if you have the money by then. If not . . .'

'Then they are yours.'

There was a glimmer of respect in Lovejoy's eyes for this woman who could be as soft as down, and yet, in protection of her family, as hard as granite.

'I do not do business this way. I do not do business this way,' Lovejoy grimaced.

Rebecca shrugged as if the transaction was over.

'But I will,' Lovejoy gabbled hurriedly.

Rebecca shot a smile of relief at Luke, who looked at his beautiful wife in admiration.

Quite a few diggers had got to know and like the

Greenwoods by now. They doffed their hats to Rebecca and hailed Luke with the usual gruff greetings.

'I almost felt sorry for the horrible man,' Rebecca chuckled. 'What an empty life he must have, with just that weird bird for family.'

'When will you be selling your bread again, Missus?' a scruffy old prospector called out.

'As soon as I get my new oven from Melbourne.'

The old prospector replaced his hat and went off muttering to himself, 'Best bread I ever tasted.'

They walked in silence for a moment, their left hands feeling oddly light and naked. 'We've really settled in here, haven't we,' Luke commented.

'Yes, it's home now. And that being the case, I'm afraid I've got a rather nasty surprise for our little savages.'

That evening, Clee, Jack and Lucy sat bolt upright in bed, outrage written all over their faces.

'Lessons!' gulped Jack.

'Yes, lessons. I hope you haven't forgotten what they are,' Rebecca said.

'You mean, like school?' Jack said.

'Exactly like school. You have been running too wild lately.'

'But who'll teach us?' asked Lucy.

'I will,' Rebecca replied.

'We were going rafting tomorrow,' Clee muttered wanly.

'You can go after your lessons. Now settle down and go to sleep.'

The children stared at one another glumly. Lucy suddenly noticed the small white pressure-mark where her mother's ring had been. 'Mum, where's your ring?'

'Oh, I've ... we've had to use it to borrow some money.'

'Why?' Lucy wanted to know.

'Because we have none left. We've used up all the money from the gold you found.'

'But haven't we found some more?' asked Jack.

'Your father hasn't had much luck. Unfortunately.'

'You must feel awful without it,' Lucy said, wide-eyed.

Rebecca had been more deeply affected by losing her ring than she had let on to Luke. She allowed some of her hurt to show through now. 'It had to be done, Lucy dear. Without it your father couldn't get another licence. And he couldn't find any more gold.'

'More gold. He hasn't found any yet,' Jack scoffed.

'That's enough, Jack,' Rebecca scolded. When Rebecca had blown out the lamp and gone, Jack lay brooding. Clee and Lucy started to whisper, as they always did. Jack felt he had to be by himself. He flung on his jacket and went out into the night.

'What's wrong now?' Clee wondered.

'Same old thing,' Lucy lamented.

Jack sat on the steps of Marcel's caravan, staring at Louis, the huge old horse. Jack would have willingly swapped places with him at the moment. It seemed a pretty good life: plenty to eat, a simple job, no school; but, best of all, you wouldn't have to think. Thinking was a headache. Thoughts of his father were wedged in his mind like splinters, and whenever he started to like Luke, it was as if they jabbed in more deeply.

Clee approached slowly. Louis snorted in greeting as she reached out to pat him. The horse watched the boy and girl, his big eyes soft in the starlight.

'Are you all right, Jack?'

'My real father would have found tons by now,' he blurted out.

'Would he?'

'Mum wouldn't have had to sell her ring.'

'I wouldn't carry on about it. She was just about crying before.'

'Yes, well she never used to cry when my father was with her. He always looked after her.'

'And so does Luke. Lucy said he looked after you all when your father died.'

'We didn't need him. I could've managed.'

'Huh! Lucy says you were starving.'

Jack dropped his eyes sulkily. 'Anyway, that was ages ago. Everybody else has had a strike here. Everybody except him.' Jack refused to soften.

'Luke is good to you, good to me, good to everybody. And you keep going on about how much of a failure he is.'

'I could've found gold by now if I wanted to,' Jack boasted.

Clee had had enough of Jack's unfair moaning. And she herself was missing her father terribly, although she never let on.

'Well, why don't you? Show us all up!' Clee gave Jack a withering look and flounced back into the tent.

Jack gazed despondently around. His eyes came to rest on Lin Ping's encampment and an idea started to form in his mind.

Lin was sitting before a small household altar, sucking on an elaborate pipe, in a haze of joss-stick smoke.

He turned around. 'Ah, come in, young Jack. Nearly finished.'

Jack sat down. He was intrigued at what Lin was doing. He had a large book open on the floor, written in Chinese script. He tossed two pennies up and noted which way they landed.

'What are you doing?'

'I am reading ... reading what cannot be seen.' Jack didn't understand. 'The future and the past and what cannot be seen in the present.'

'How do you do that?'

'With the "I Ching". This book and these pennies.'

'Can you read my future?' Jack inquired.

'Have done so already. All your family. You a strange mixture. Pretend to be a fighter but you are not fighter. Really a gentle person. In the future you will be soft. like water.'

Jack stared around the room, trying to come to terms with its foreignness. There were Chinese prayer-scrolls and paper lanterns with dragons on them and oddly painted wall-hangings everywhere.

'And what about Luke?'

'Luke is violent man who has become gentle. He has done much fighting in past ... but it is now over.'

'Are you sure?' frowned Jack.

'The "I Ching" tells me,' Lin nodded. 'But you did not come about the future or the past. But the present. What is it, Jack?'

'Um, I want to find some gold.'

'We all want that.'

'Do you know of any place, which hasn't been mined before, where there might be some?'

'If I knew of such a place I would be there myself.'

'You seem to know a lot of things you don't let on about.'

Lin smiled and bowed. 'There is place I know. but far from river. So, very hard to wash dirt with water. But I think gold could be there.'

Jack smiled his thanks, as the old Chinaman seemed to dissolve and reappear through the swirling joss and pipe fumes and the stuttering light.

The sun was beating down on to the tent. The children were not usually cooped up inside at mid-morning, but today was different. Today was the first day of school. Jack was dying with impatience, chafing to get down to the place that Lin had told him about.

'That's short division. Now what is long division?' Rebecca gazed at her unwilling pupils. Nobody answered. 'Jack, you would have done it at school in Melbourne.'

'Um . . .' Jack racked his brains.

'Well, tell the class how it's done.'

'Um . . . I must've been away that day, I think.'

Rebecca sighed and surveyed her listless pupils. 'Well, say you want to divide five hundred and seventy-six by twenty-four. How would you go about that?'

Once again, there was a deafening silence.

Rebecca clicked her tongue in annoyance. Her eyes lighted on the table covered with flour on which she kneaded the dough for the bread. She spread some more flour over it and traced the sum. The stifling atmosphere in the tent and the dusty flour made Jack want to sneeze. Rebecca gave him a warning look. His eyes began to water.

'Now our first step is to see if twenty-four goes into fifty-seven.'

Jack was swiftly overcome with a huge sneeze. The flour

was blown away and the sum obliterated. Rebecca pursed her lips as the girls started giggling.

Jack looked apologetically at her. 'Hay-fever,' he sniffed.

'Mischief, more like,' shouted Rebecca as she snatched up a broom and chased him out of the tent.

'This is the spot Lin told me about.' Sean looked doubtfully at where Jack was standing, then in the direction of the river, calculating.

'But how are we going to wash the dirt?'

'We'll have to bring the water from the river.' Jack was resolute and eager to get started. He unshouldered a sack with the pick-shovel and panning dish in it.

'Why don't we take the dirt to the river?' asked Clee.

'It'll be just as much trouble,' Sean said.

'What about Louis?' Clee suggested.

Jack and Sean regarded her approvingly, stopping short of congratulation, since both of them were annoyed that it hadn't been their brainwave. Clee went to fetch Louis while Jack and Sean fashioned some pannier-bags out of ropes and old sacks. Presently, Clee reappeared leading the old horse.

'You're just about clever enough to be a man, Clee.' Sean said generously.

'Thanks very much,' said Clee.

Jack was in no mood for mucking around. 'Sean and I will do the digging. You girls, hold open the bags.' Jack's tone had become quite dictatorial. The others exchanged irritated looks.

Jack grabbed the pick and slammed it into the earth. 'Well, come on.'

'They're trying to abolish slavery, you know,' Sean said

dryly. Jack ignored this and continued hacking at the ground as though he hated it. Bojinda appeared, as he always did, silently and seemingly from nowhere, with his usual litheness and economy of effort. He regarded their toil askance.

'Hey, Bojinda, you better not let Jack see you loafing, he'll murder you,' Clee shouted.

Bojinda smiled his huge smile, not understanding. Jack kept on working.

'Make yourself useful, Bojinda. Rustle up some lunch,' Sean called. Bojinda shrugged and went off to forage.

Down by the river, Jack emptied the paydirt out of the sacks into his dish. He stared hopefully into the bottom of it, but there was nothing. He grunted in disgust and repeated the procedure. Louis happily cropped the succulent grass behind him. Jack worked feverishly. He'd show everybody just how useless Luke was. He, Jack, could look after Lucy and Rebecca without any help from an outsider. He'd show everybody ... So Jack was searching as much for a way out of the emotional trap he had dug himself as for the tiny grains of yellow.

When Jack returned from the river, he found that Bojinda had prepared lunch. The aborigine had collected a huge bark-basket full of witchetty grubs. He had skewered three or four on a number of sticks and they were roasting over a small fire.

'You want eat?'

The white youngsters approached gingerly. They observed the wriggling mass of fat white bodies and the others turning golden brown, sizzling over the fire. They swallowed queasily, trying to put out of their minds how similar to giant maggots the larvae looked.

Bojinda led by example; he pulled one off the skewer and tossed it into his mouth with great relish. He proffered the stick to Sean who reluctantly took one. Closing his eyes, he popped the grub into his mouth. He chewed cautiously as though his teeth were made of egg-shell. But then a relieved smile spread across his face and he reached for another.

Before long, they were all gobbling down the fat white grubs as fast as Bojinda could cook them. How strange it was, Lucy thought, that a short time ago they had lived in a crowded city street full of over-dressed people and harsh metallic noises, and now they sat on the earth with an aborigine, munching worms, with the pollen-laden wind eddying about them.

Before long, Jack started to grow restless. He gazed disapprovingly at the little progress they had made with their digging. 'All right, let's get back to it.'

There were groans of protest. 'We're not convict labour,' Sean complained.

'If we want to find some gold, we've got to keep at it,' Jack said unrepentantly. And he led the way back to the excavation. The others exchanged a look of annoyance and went to join him.

Clee and Lucy were really glad to get into bed that night. They ached in every limb after the unaccustomed work.

Rebecca looked at their dirty clothes and frowned. 'How do you get your clothes so filthy?'

'Um . . . It's all the mud around,' Jack replied weakly.

'But most people step over the mud, Jack, they don't roll around in it. I don't know what Marcel will say when he comes back. You're turning Clee into a little savage like yourselves.' She surveyed the three apologetic faces peering over the rough blankets and smiled despite herself. 'And don't forget your prayers.'

But before Clee said her prayers, she had something to settle with Jack. 'Lucy and I don't want to do any digging tomorrow, Jack.'

'We'd rather go for a ride on the raft,' Lucy added.

'Well, that's too bad. You've got to help,' Jack replied shortly.

'You're not our boss, you know,' Lucy retorted.

Jack propped himself up on one elbow. He was getting angry. 'Listen, we need the money. Don't you understand that?'

'That's not why you want to find the gold,' Lucy said.

'Isn't it?'

'It's because you want to prove that you're better than Father,' Lucy said agitatedly.

'My father's dead.'

'Oh, don't start that again,' Clee groaned.

'Luke's your father and he's a good father, only you're too stupid to see it,' Lucy said forlornly.

Jack stared at his little sister through the gloom. He knew deep down that there was truth in what she said. But to let even a little bit of truth in would threaten the lies he had to tell himself to keep his dead father alive and his live father dead. He knew the best way to silence her – too bad if it was cruel. 'At least I haven't forgotten my real father.'

Lucy went quiet.

'Lucy hasn't either, Jack. She's doing what has to be done.'

'And what's that?'

Clee wasn't sure how to put it. When her mother had left,

she had cried herself to sleep for months. But eventually she'd learnt that some things cannot be changed, no matter how much you wish them to be otherwise; and it is silly to torture yourself with what can never be. 'You . . . you . . . can't keep on going back,' she finally said.

Jack was about to make a stinging retort to this, but the sound of Lucy's soft weeping made the words turn to ash in his mouth. He turned to the wall to sleep and hoped with all his heart that he would not dream again that night.

What had passed between them was not spoken of again as next day they tramped back to the pit they had dug the day before. But Jack no longer barked orders at the girls; indeed, it seemed he was determined to do all the work himself. As soon as they arrived, he jumped into the hole and began to dig as if there would be no tomorrow. The girls shovelled the shingly soil into the pannier-bags.

Sean noticed how deeply Jack had dug into the side of the hill. He was worried. 'Hey, it's time to put some timber supports in.'

Jack stopped and inspected the sides of the hole. 'No, it'll be all right for a bit. I want to keep going.'

'I'm telling you, it needs shoring. It's dangerous.'

'Don't worry. I'll give you a shout when I'm ready to put them in.'

So firm was Jack's reply that Sean shook his head and walked away.

Jack carried on as though the devil was driving him. He didn't see the overhang shift slightly, and small cracks appear in it. His first warning was a trickle of soil down his back and he looked up to see the sky blotted out.

The others turned around after the huge crash, just in time

to see tons of rock and dirt settling. Lucy started to scream.

'I told him,' Sean grunted as he clawed at the debris. The three of them scrabbled at the rock-fall, trying to clear the stones away.

'Jack! Jack! Jack!' shrieked Lucy frantically.

Clee heard a groan. She strained her ears. There it was again. She held her hand up for the others to stop.

A muttered groan filtered out of a chink in the rock pile. 'I'm here. I'm here.' They followed the direction of his voice and scrambled over.

Clee caught a glimpse of him through the chink. 'There. There he is. Through here.' And sure enough Jack lay, covered with soil and stones, behind a barrier of a dozen big boulders.

'Are you hurt?' Sean asked.

'Don't think so. Just can't move at all.' Then they saw why: Jack was buried up to his neck.

'Hang on. We'll soon get you out of there.' Sean grabbed a boulder and tried to shift it, but it was too big for him. He managed to move a smaller one, and Lucy and Clee working together moved another.

'Don't worry, Jack. We'll get you out,' Lucy cried.

Jack gave a watery smile. Then, without warning, there was another small rock-fall, and Jack's face became covered.

'Jack! Jack!' Lucy screamed desperately.

'Hang on, Jack!'

'He can't breathe! He can't breathe!' Lucy was almost hysterical.

Without hesitation, Clee tried to wriggle herself into the small opening. 'I'm coming, Jack!' Using all her fairground skills, she squirmed through the small gap, but her hips jammed. 'Sean, give me a shove.'

'The whole hill could come down,' Sean shouted.

'Give me a shove!' Reluctantly, Sean did so. 'Harder!' And she popped through. She scraped the earth from Jack's face.

He emerged, gasping and spluttering and choking; he sucked lungfuls of air in. Lucy and Sean applauded as Clee dug with her hands to get Jack out.

'Thanks. Thank you Cleopatre,' said Jack.

'I knew you would come in handy sooner or later,' Sean joked with relief. Clee reached for Jack's hand and gave it a squeeze.

Sean and Lucy pulled at the wall of stone and dirt. There were two big boulders which they could not budge. However, Sean made a harness out of rope and Louis dragged them away effortlessly. Clee and Jack crawled out.

Lucy hugged her brother very hard. 'Jack, are you all right? Did you get hurt?'

'I'm fine, Lucy.' Jack was shaken and pale, but no lasting damage had been done. All of a sudden, however, his eyes widened and his mouth fell open; he looked as though he was about to have a fit. Then they spotted the cause of his behaviour: the rock-fall had brought with it a huge gold nugget.

Jack picked it up, crowing with delight. 'Look, we've done it! Whoopee!'

The others crowded around to stroke the dull yellow lump. Soon they were screeching with joy.

Not far away, Ernest and Bones sat under a tree surrounded by torn-open purses and rifled wallets. Their horses were tethered nearby, still breathing heavily after the gallop away from the hold-up.

'We'll have to give it up unless the travelling public improve. Bones. Thirty lousy bob.' Bones nodded morosely and hurled a wallet into the bushes.

Suddenly they heard young voices screaming with delight. Mystified, Ernest rose and waved Bones to follow him. From the hilltop, they were astounded to witness the children dancing around exultantly.

'How much do you reckon it's worth?' Sean asked.

'It weighs about ... at least three pounds,' Jack crowed.

'So that's nearly ... um ... a lot of money. anyway,' said Sean, his arithmetic giving up on him.

'We're rich, we're rich,' Clee rejoiced.

'We shouldn't tell Mum and Dad until we've found some more,' Lucy suggested.

'Yes, good idea.'

Back on the hilltop, Ernest's eyes hung out like organ-stops. 'Did you see the size of it?'

Bones nodded greedily. Ernest licked his unshaven lips, drooling like a dog over meat.

The bandits stood before Lovejoy. He could scarcely believe his ears. 'Those children are totally undeserving.'

'Especially that one with the limp,' Ernest rasped.

'Now we must have a plan,' Lovejoy said cunningly.

'Why don't we just slit their throats,' Ernest suggested.

Bones shook his head in alarm.

'Ernest, I am a businessman, not a criminal,' Lovejoy said. 'Why murder or steal when you can get what you want within the law?'

'Nobody would ever find out. We'd bury them in their own hole.' Ernest chuckled gruesomely.

'Listen, you oaf, if their parents don't know what they're doing, they couldn't possibly have a miner's licence. In any case they can hardly afford one, let alone two. So don't you see . . . ?'

Ernest furrowed his brow as he tried to work out what Lovejoy was getting at. 'You mean, we kill their parents as well?'

'No! *We* get a licence in the morning and it becomes our claim.'

Ernest followed the sense of this at last. He looked at Lovejoy in admiration. To get what you want without murder or robbery . . . so that's what education does for you.

Rebecca looked at the children sitting around the dinner table, unable to read their mood. They were drum-tight with triumph and yet were trying not to show it.

She threw a glance at Luke. 'Did something happen today?'

'We just had some fun down by the river, didn't we?' said Jack evasively.

'Yes, we just mucked around with Sean,' Clee agreed.

'And had another roll in the mud, by the look of your clothes,' Rebecca scolded.

The youngsters looked guiltily down at their dirty clothing. 'I don't mind washing them myself, Mum.' Jack offered.

'And I'll hang them out to dry,' Clee joined in.

Curiouser and curiouser. Neither Jack nor Clee usually volunteered to do household chores.

'We must try this wallowing in mud, Luke. It certainly has improved their temper, don't you think?'

'Perhaps it's the schoolwork which has put them in such a good mood,' Luke joked.

The children groaned, but not half as loudly as when Rebecca added, 'Yes, you're right. I bet they're really looking forward to Tables and Spelling tomorrow.'

The children walked springily towards their diggings. Jack was whistling, despite the fact that he had a sore head from having slept on the gold nugget under his pillow. Lucy smiled to herself. She hadn't seen Jack this happy for a long time.

They all bumped into Sean who had suddenly stopped stock-still. They followed the direction of his horrified gaze, and all took off down the slope together.

'That's ours,' Sean bellowed.

'Hey, what do you think you're doing?' Jack yelled.

Bones and Ernest straightened from their digging, and Lovejoy folded his arms and awaited the arrival of the outraged youngsters.

'I should've known, old Killjoy himself,' Sean observed.

'That's our claim. We were here before you,' Jack screamed.

'Don't shout at me, kid, it gives me a headache,' Ernest hissed.

'This is our claim,' piped Lucy.

'Why don't you push off,' Clee added for good measure.

Enraged, Jack raced around the three men, and Ernest made a grab for him. Lovejoy stilled him with a gesture. 'So this is your claim, is it? If that's the case, you won't mind showing us your miner's licence, will you?'

'You're a villain, Lovejoy, and so are you two,' Jack spluttered with frustration.

'Why so bashful? I'm not afraid to show you my licence,' Lovejoy boasted, pulling it out and displaying it. 'Signed, sealed and delivered. So leave my claim at once.'

'You're ... dirty claim-jumpers,' Jack spluttered.

Sean put his arm around the boy and led him away. He didn't want Jack getting too close to Ernest, whose hand was hovering dangerously over the large knife sheathed in his belt. 'Jack, he's right. If we haven't filed a claim, that's that.'

Even Lucy was furious. As they retreated she called back over her shoulder, 'You're all horrible. And I hate you.' The youngsters left with a last longing look at their lost El Dorado.

Lovejoy's dry chuckle of triumph sounded like Satan's own laugh. He turned to his henchmen. 'Now dig!' But Ernest and Bones hated honest employment as much as a cat hates a bath.

After a little more digging, Ernest suddenly threw down his shovel. 'There's no gold here, Uriah. Those dratted kids must have got the only bit.'

'I'm not doing any more,' Bones grunted, sitting down.

'We're bushrangers, not miners. We steal, we don't work for our living,' Ernest proclaimed.

Lovejoy had no way of forcing them to do his bidding. Anyway, he felt thoroughly miserable outside in the fresh air and broad daylight. He longed to get back into his dim store and have a chat with Jasper.

Rebecca and Luke could hardly believe their eyes as they stared at the wrinkled nugget of gold on the table.

'It's huge.'

'We could've got a lot more   Jack said.

'And you could've got hurt, Luke replied gently.

Jack, Clee and Lucy nodded. That much was true.

'Well at least the mystery of the dirty clothes is solved,' Rebecca grinned.

'And Jack is right, Dad,' put in Lucy. 'Lovejoy is a villain. He must be, to be friends with those wicked men.'

'All the more reason to keep away from them. Lucy. But don't get me wrong, Jack. I am very proud of you ... all of you. Except, I'd rather we had to eat grass than that any of you was hurt ... even a little bit.' Luke smiled at Jack with love and caring.

And for the first time Jack didn't turn away. He tried to smile back and, although his attempt was not perfect, it didn't make his face ache at all. And then he heard himself saying, as if somebody else was using his mouth, 'The first thing I'd like to do with my share of the money is get back your wedding rings.' Lucy and Clee acclaimed this loudly.

Rebecca looked from her son to her husband. It was the first sign that the thaw had set in.

It could be felt in the air and on the skin. The wind was no longer sharpened in the Antarctic. The sun seemed to be taking its job more seriously and was rousing itself higher and higher. Summer waited just around the corner.

The Greenwoods marched up the main street, relishing in advance Lovejoy's turmoil when they showed him the hunk of gold. Jack and Clee brought up the rear. 'I think it was really nice of you to want to get their rings back,' Clee smiled.

Jack was still stumped as to where the idea had come from. He didn't want it to be seen as a sign of weakness or surrender. 'I'm only doing it because I know Lovejoy wants to keep the rings.'

Clee looked around at him. But she realized that he wasn't telling the whole truth. 'No, you're not. You want your father and mother to be happy.'

Jack assumed his toughest expression, shrugged his shoulders and kicked a stone.

'Don't you?' She shoved him hard. Jack stumbled and his tough expression cracked into a grin. 'You're not as tough as you make out, Jack Greenwood.'

CHAPTER
SEVEN

A fishing-line dangled into the river. Lucy held it lightly so as to feel the bite. Bojinda sat in his customary position, cross-legged and motionless, his black eyes unblinking. Jack and Clee lolled about on the bank, and Sean sat dozing with his back against the tree. Bojinda was telling them a legend.

'In the dreaming, there was no river. A big kangaroo spirit here. He very proud and could jump very high. He have three sons and one day he say to them, "I jump as high as the sun."' Bojinda made a bouncing motion towards the sun and, throughout the rest of his story, he illustrated the movements with his arms and hands. 'His wife asked him not to do it in case it angered the sun spirit. But he jumped so high he knocked some pieces off the sun and these fell ... and set on fire. Everything was burnt up. Even his family. He was very sorry and lay down to die. He began to weep. But as punishment, he has never died but weep ever since and this river in our talking is called "The Kangaroo's Tears", because all this water is his tears.'

Bojinda had told the story well and the children were enthralled. They looked at the river with new eyes.

'And this is why the gold you dig up causes so much bad luck and fighting.'

'Why?' Jack inquired.

'Because gold is piece of sun and not to be touched.'

'And your tribe have known about the gold all along?' Clee asked.

Bojinda nodded.

Lucy suddenly tensed and motioned them to be quiet. The line in her fingers was being tugged.

'Have you got a bite?' Clee whispered.

Lucy nodded. Her line suddenly zig-zagged through the water and she began to haul it in. There was much excitement and advice from the others.

'It must be a big one. It's pulling very hard,' Lucy commented excitedly.

And it was a big one. It broke the surface, still full of fight. But Lucy pulled it on to the bank hand over hand, where it lay flapping and struggling.

'Well done, Lucy.'

'What a whopper!'

But Bojinda was not so pleased. He drew back from where the fish lay flapping and gasping on the ground.

'What's wrong, Bojinda?' Clee asked.

'This fish no good.'

'Why?'

'This fish – he got bad spirit inside.'

Sean grasped the fish and worked the hook out of its mouth. He picked up a stick and whacked it on the back of the head. It twitched and lay still. 'What sort of bad spirit?' he demanded.

'If you eat, you get sick.'

The white youngsters thought about this. They glanced over at the fish. It gave one last feeble flick of its tail.

'I've eaten them lots of times. And I'm all right,' Sean contradicted Bojinda.

'Now you are,' Bojinda said flatly. The children stared once more at the big black fish, wondering.

However, hunger had little trouble defeating their misgivings, and they built a fire and roasted it in the hot embers. Bojinda wanted no part in it and stalked away.

They raked the fish out of the embers, wrapped it in leaves and took it up to their tree-hut to dine in comfort. They peeled back the skin and tucked into the tasty flesh. Soon there was nothing left but the skeleton.

They lay back, licking their fingers.

'If only we'd had some spuds,' Sean belched.

'I've never seen Bojinda so upset. Do you reckon it's true?' Clee mused.

'We're still alive, aren't we?' Sean pooh-poohed the notion.

'It was really delicious,' said Lucy, sucking her teeth.

They heard the sound of galloping hooves approaching and stopped talking. Bones and Ernest rode into view and allowed their horses to walk up and drink from the river. The youngsters held their breath, terrified that the bushrangers would look up and discover them.

'So the coach will come through that valley,' Ernest bubbled with delight.

'It's got to.'

'And next Tuesday it will be loaded with gold.'

'That's what I was told.'

The youngsters exchanged sober looks as the seriousness of what was being discussed sank in.

'Bones, I reckon after this one we'll be able to retire. And you'll be able to go back and live with your mother,' Ernest said with uncharacteristic pleasantness. Bones smiled in agreement.

When their horses had drunk their fill, the bushrangers cantered off.

Danks had just received a letter from Melbourne. It concerned Luke: the circuit magistrate had taken an interest in the case and would be in Jericho soon. Luke would be charged and tried. Danks smirked with satisfaction. At that moment, Jack and Clee burst into his office. Jack began, 'Officer Danks, we've ...'

'Be quiet!'

'But we've just heard ...'

'Silence, boy, or I'll clap you in irons!'

'But you don't understand. We overheard ...' Clee chimed in.

'And you'll go with him.' He fixed them with an evil look until they settled down. He returned to reading the document in front of him. Finally he raised his eyes. 'Now, what is it you have to tell me?'

'We heard the two bushrangers talking about robbing the coach next Tuesday.'

'Which bushrangers?'

'You know, Lovejoy's friends,' Clee informed him

'Hold your tongues! I will not listen to this slander. Mr Lovejoy is a law-abiding citizen.'

'But they're definitely planning to rob the coach on Tuesday.'

'You're sure that's what you heard?'

A smug look settled on Danks' face. Jack sensed that the question was an ambush. He nodded slowly.

'Well, that's odd, because there's no coach coming to Jericho next Tuesday,' Danks told them triumphantly.

'Are you sure?' Clee queried.

'Don't be cheeky with me, young lady. Why don't you run along and play your little games without upsetting the grown-ups.'

'It's not a game!' Jack exclaimed.

'First you accuse Mr Lovejoy of stealing your father's wallet ... now this. If you waste my time again I will do something about it.'

Jack and Clee lowered their eyes. Why were grown-ups so stupid?

They walked slowly home. Rebecca was outside with the travelling merchant. He had just unloaded Rebecca's new cast-iron oven and two huge barrels of flour. Clee's humour was totally restored when the grizzled old merchant held out an envelope and asked who 'Mademwazelle Duberau' was. Clee grabbed the letter, almost forgetting to thank him. She scooted off to read it. Jack was very pleased to be invited along.

Clee sat on the magic chest inside the caravan and tore open the envelope. Jack flopped on to the bed and listened as she read it aloud.

'*Ma Chérie*, thank you for sending me all that money. You were very clever to find the gold. I have now only twenty-five pounds to pay back to get out of this cursed place. If I do not pay, my trial has been set for the end of this month. I thank God that we were lucky enough to meet the Greenwood family. I pray also that He will keep you safe. I think of you constantly. Your loving Papa.'

Clee folded the letter carefully, trying to control her quivering lips.

'Luke said the next gold we find will go straight to Melbourne to pay off his debt,' Jack said.

Clee smiled sadly at this. She glanced around at all the costumes and sideshow bits and pieces which reminded her so painfully of her father.

Jack put his hand on her shoulder. 'He will be back soon. You'll see.'

Clee shook her head to dispel the gloom; she tried to smile. and, although a little crooked at first, the smile grew brighter as she realized what a good friend she had in Jack.

Lucy had been looking for Jack and Clee down by the river. She was returning home to see if they were there, when she started to feel very peculiar. She couldn't work out what was happening to her: her head thumped and was very hot, but the rest of her felt quite cold. The distance between her and the encampment seemed to be getting longer with each heavy step ... And something odd was happening to their house. It started to hover above the ground. Her legs felt wobbly as she reached the yard. She looked up at the sky to make sure the sun was still there, because everything was getting dark and cold. Jack appeared hazy and shimmering, then the earth seemed to open up and swallow her. 'Jack.' she croaked.

Jack rushed over, calling for his mother. Lucy's lips were parched and her face chalky.

Rebecca rushed out of the house, wiping her floury hands on her apron. She knelt down by Lucy's side. 'Lucy ... Lucy ... What's the matter?' She cradled her head.

Lucy's eyes flickered open. Her tongue was swollen and she could not move it. She smiled sweetly and slipped into unconsciousness.

Jack sprinted off to fetch Doc Slope. His lame leg thudded painfully into the ground but he did not heed it.

Doc took Lucy's temperature and felt her pulse. The larger-than-life Mississippi man, so flamboyant when holding forth on politics or photography, was quiet and dedicated when treating the sick. He looked up slowly. His face was very worried. He smoothed the blankets down around the motionless girl.

'I'm afraid to say that she has typhoid fever.'

Rebecca closed her eyes in despair. 'Oh, Doctor, couldn't it be something else.'

'I've seen too much of it not to know the signs.' He fetched a bottle of his famous elixir out of his bag. 'Give her some of this as soon as she wakes and make sure she gets plenty to drink.'

'Is it bad, Doc, really?'

'I'm afraid we can only hope.'

Jack felt as if an icy hand had closed around his heart and squeezed.

Later that day, Clee, Jack, Sean and Ted who had become increasingly friendly lately, sat outside the house. Ted had challenged them to a game of marbles. He flicked a marble skilfully and knocked one of Jack's out of the ring drawn in the dust. 'How do you like that! What a great shot!' The others stared back at him, unable to summon up any enthusiasm. 'Come on, Jack, it's your go.'

Jack heard Ted's voice as if from a hundred sad miles away. 'Uh? Oh, look, Ted, I don't feel like playing.'

'Hey, Lucy's in there sick as can be. Nobody wants to play,' Sean told Ted off gently. Ted looked disappointed till this information sank in, then he nodded and sat down with the others. Clee drew blindly in the dust with a stick. Jack shook his head as if to throw off some of the tension of waiting.

Suddenly Bojinda arrived, walking with his effortless gait, as if materializing out of thin air. 'Want to see Lucy,' he announced.

'She's sick, Bojinda.'

'That's why I want to see her.'

'But how did you know?' Clee asked.

'She sick because she eat the spirit fish. Let me see her. I try to help.'

Jack, Clee and Bojinda entered quietly.

Lucy was in the grip of a high fever. She twisted and turned, trying to ease her racked limbs. Rebecca sponged her forehead with a wet cloth. Luke was pressing oranges and collecting their juice in a jug. Each time Lucy moaned, he winced, almost as though it was *his* pain. Jack observed how much Luke cared for his step-daughter.

Lucy was having the most hideous dream. She dreamt that she was swimming in the river. The day was blisteringly hot and the water was steaming. Suddenly she started to sink and she called out for help. Luke came to her rescue, and as he was taking her back to the shore a huge black fish swam towards them. It started to bite Luke. But the most horrible part of the dream was that the fish had Jack's face, twisted with hate. Then it began to bite and tear at *her*. She moaned. 'Jack . . . Jack . . . Daddy loves you. Don't hurt me. Don't hurt me. Jack, Daddy . . . loves . . . you.'

Everybody in the tent stared at the delirious girl, her back arched as if trying to escape from something. Jack was horrified. It was as though somebody had read his most secret thoughts and was shouting them out loud. He glanced over to Luke, who was staring at him gravely.

Jack tip-toed across to Rebecca. 'Mum. Bojinda says he wants to sit with Lucy for a while. Is that all right?' Rebecca nodded to Bojinda.

He moved to the bedside. Then he made some sort of sign on Lucy's forehead and muttered something in his own language. He sat down on the ground and started chanting softly, his body swaying as he became more and more immersed in the prayer. The slanting rays of the setting sun fell on his black skin and made it glimmer.

Lin entered, carrying a Chinese teapot. He handed it to Rebecca. 'This is Chinese herbs. To take away fever.' Rebecca took the pot and smiled her thanks. 'You do me honour to accept. How is dear Lucy?'

'No change,' Rebecca said softly.

'Ah. So sorry.'

They all gazed at Bojinda. He looked quite unreal in the failing light. He seemed to be in some sort of trance. Lin nodded slowly as if he understood.

Lucy felt as if she was rising up from some vast depth. She looked up through the water, no longer stained with blood, and made out Bojinda swimming above her. He reached down and grabbed her hair, as before, and hauled her out. At last she could breathe good, clean air again.

The next day, Clee and Jack walked miserably along the outskirts of the goldfields. It was a blustery day but the wind was warm with pledges of summer and laden with scent from the bud-burst in the bush. However, they were too wrapped up in their own sad thoughts to pay much attention to nature.

'If Lucy gets well I'm never going to be unkind to her again. I'm really horrible to her sometimes,' Jack confessed.

Clee nodded and they walked on in silence for a short distance.

'Do you think it was really the fish that has made her sick?' Clee wondered.

'I don't know. Before we came here I wouldn't have believed it. But now ... since I've met Bojinda ...' Jack shrugged.

'Nobody told him about Lucy being sick, but he knew,' said Clee. Jack nodded, as puzzled as she was. 'It was strange what the fever made her say, wasn't it?' Clee said probingly.

Jack recalled the words very well. They were branded on to his mind; but he didn't want to talk about it. He shrugged.

'She said you're hurting her by not loving Luke.'

Jack knew that this was true. He quickened his pace as if to escape it.

Clee hurried after him and clamped her hand on to his arm. She tried to make Jack look at her but he wouldn't. 'You're hurting everybody, Jack, but Lucy most of all.' This struck home. Clee let go. He still would not look at her.

They had stopped at the edge of a flooded prospecting pit. Jack picked up a stone and flung it into the middle of the pond. As they watched, perfect circles rippled to the edges and stopped at their feet.

When they returned to the Greenwood yard, Bojinda was sitting in the dust, chanting quietly. Jack called out to him, but he did not seem to hear. They waited for a while, but eventually went inside.

Doc was taking Lucy's pulse. He had one hand on her wrist and in the other he held his big fob-watch. He frowned deeply. He then checked the glands in her neck. He was very perplexed. Rebecca and Luke were on tenterhooks as they craned forward, fearing that Doc's mystification meant a worsening in her condition.

'Well, dang me! Amazing. Quite extraordinary.' Jack and Clee stood quietly in the corner, agog to know what Doc meant. He turned from the sick-bed. 'I'll be horn-swaggled. In all my experience as a physician and surgeon – on two continents, remember – I have never seen typhoid fever cured so quickly.'

'You mean she's getting better?' Rebecca breathed.

'That's exactly what I mean, Ma'am. And I must say I cannot explain it.'

'Praise the Lord,' Luke gasped joyfully.

'I can only deduce that my famous elixir has had something to do with this miraculous recovery.' Clee and Jack smiled.

Lucy stirred, groaned and blinked awake. The others stepped forward happily. She took a moment to get her bearings and then recognized those around her.

'You're going to be all right,' Rebecca cried, embracing her joyfully.

Lucy made a big effort to speak. 'Bojinda ...'

'What's that, darling?'

'Where's Bojinda?' Lucy muttered. Luke nodded to Jack, instructing him to go and fetch Bojinda.

'I must write an article on this for the American Medical

Journal. They're always glad to publish me,' Doc said airily, his thumbs in his waistcoat.

Jack and Bojinda came in. At the sight of her aborigine friend, Lucy's face lit up and she extended her hand. Bojinda moved to the bedside. They clasped each other's hands firmly.

'Thank you, Bojinda. Thank you.' Bojinda stared at her gravely. Jack looked at their hands, joined together like a black and white knot.

The coach-driver stuck his hands in the air as he felt the cold muzzle of Ernest's gun press against his temple. Ernest had jumped up as the coach slowed down to cross a ford. He pulled on the reins and the horses came to a halt.

'Now tell the guard to come out,' he whispered fiercely.

'Ah, Reg, could you step out here for a bit?'

The guard opened the carriage door and got out. Bones padded up behind him with a rifle and disarmed him. The guard was taken completely by surprise and could do nothing.

'Now, if you both want to eat supper tonight, do exactly what I tell you,' Ernest ordered them. 'Load the strongbox on to that pack-horse.' The guard and the driver staggered under the weight of the box. This made Ernest's eyes dance with pleasure.

'It's nice and heavy, Ernie.'

'Don't call me Ernie.' Bones did not seem to understand. 'In front of witnesses, you idiot,' Ernest hissed.

Bones thought about this and nodded as if he understood. 'Sorry, Ernest.'

Ernest rolled his eyes in exasperation. Bones lashed the box on to the pack-horse. 'Now we're all going to wait here until my friend gets a good start,' Ernest declared jauntily.

Bones rode off, leading the pack-horse.

'Lovely day, isn't it?' Ernest chuckled.

'It'll be just this sort of day when they hang you,' the driver said.

'Is that any way to talk to a man with a gun pointed at your heart?'

Jack and Clee sauntered down the main street, feeling on top of the world. Sean had got a job working at the stables. They went to see him and told him of Lucy's astonishing recovery. Sean was very pleased: 'I reckon that's enough work for the time being. Let's have a wander.' Jack loved wandering around with Sean. Something exciting always seemed to happen.

The thunder of the approaching coach was heard. It rounded the corner and rushed down the street. The horses were wide-eyed and champing at the bit. The youngsters jogged up as the driver descended from the platform, screaming blue murder.

'We've been robbed again. Bushrangers, the same two. This time they got the Creswick gold!' As he strode towards the watchhouse, Danks hurried out, buttoning up his tunic.

'But ... But you're not due till tomorrow,' Danks stammered.

'From Ballarat, we're not. But we did a special run to pick up the gold from Creswick.'

'We told him it was coming on Tuesday, didn't we?' Jack said. Clee and Sean nodded.

'They were the same two as last time. What do you do all day, play cards?' the driver bellowed.

'Now look here. I am responsible for a huge area, from Creswick right down to Kalangamite Gorge. I've asked for another man, but it's no good.'

As the youngsters moved away, Danks' apologies grew fainter.

'Time for a council of war, I reckon,' Sean announced solemnly. All discussion of important matters took place at the tree-hut. There was something about the rustling leaves and smell of water which cleared the head. And, more importantly, no grown-ups were likely to intrude and spoil things.

'Danks must be on their side. Otherwise how come they haven't been caught?' Sean began.

'I don't know that he's just part of the gang. Isn't he just stupid?' Clee said.

'I reckon he's turning a blind eye to them. Look how he is with Lovejoy. Lovejoy can do no wrong,' Sean replied.

'I reckon it's up to us to get those bushrangers,' Jack said stoutly.

'But how? We don't even know where they come from.'

'We've got to make Lovejoy tell us,' Jack declared darkly.

'Lovejoy! He wouldn't tell us what time of day it was,' Sean scoffed.

They pondered for a moment, staring into the river for inspiration.

'We could grab Jasper and threaten to kill him unless Lovejoy told us,' Jack suggested.

'Yes! He really loves that bird,' Sean agreed.

'And would we kill him?' Clee wanted to know.

'You bet,' said Jack unhesitatingly.

'He deserves it. He's evil,' Sean said.

'Then what do we do?' Jack asked.

'Food!' Clee exclaimed. The boys had no idea what she meant. Obviously she had dismissed the previous suggestion. 'Food! Those bushrangers have got to eat, haven't they?'

The boys nodded, not sure where this was leading.

'Well, Lovejoy must take out supplies sometimes. We'll have to keep watch. We can see the track from here.'

'What if he goes when we're not watching?' asked Jack.

'Have you got a better idea?' Clee retorted.

'You two take first watch. I've got to get back to work,' Sean said, as he started to climb down the tree. 'Make an arrow with some sticks, pointing which way he's gone.'

Rebecca tucked Lucy in, then bent down and kissed her on the forehead. She was now sleeping deeply and wholesomely. Luke was sitting, mending the handle of a shovel.

'The fever's completely gone,' Rebecca observed.

'We're very fortunate,' Luke said happily.

Rebecca walked over to where Luke was sitting and put her hands on his shoulders. 'I'm glad you let Bojinda say his prayers . . . or spells or whatever they were.'

'There was no reason to stop him.'

'Even though they were . . . well . . . pagan,' Rebecca said.

Luke smiled and shrugged as he fastened the broken handle with twine.

'We've all changed out here, haven't we?' Rebecca mused.

'We've had to.'

'I wonder what *did* help Lucy . . . I mean, the doctor felt that his elixir did the trick. Then there was that odd-smelling herbal tea which Lin gave us. Then there was Bojinda's ... black magic ... was it?'

'I don't know what you'd call it,' Luke puzzled.

'The children say that Bojinda blames her illness on an evil fish she ate.'

'I suppose he could be right. After all, we know almost nothing about the creatures in this country. And Doc said typhoid fever is carried by the river.'

'Then there were your own prayers ... and love,' said Rebecca, as they both gazed blissfully at their healthy, sleeping daughter.

'Lucy was convinced it was Bojinda,' Luke said.

Rebecca nodded her head wondering, 'Perhaps it was a combination of good wills.'

'And perhaps my prayers and Bojinda's go to the same God,' Luke nodded thoughtfully.

'The friends we've made here are far more valuable than the gold we've found,' Rebecca remarked.

Luke had finished mending the shovel. He set it aside and sighed heavily. 'I just wish I could make friends with my own son.'

Rebecca took Luke's hand in hers. She understood how much he had suffered at Jack's rejection. But they both knew there was nothing they could do. All the processes of healing are mysterious, as they had just seen, but the healing of a grieving heart was the most mysterious of all.

Jack and Clee stared out across the bush in one direction, then over Jericho in the other. The diggers were foraging and burrowing away like ants.

'We'd better go back soon,' Clee said.

Jack looked at the sun. It was late afternoon. 'We'll wait a bit. The evenings are getting longer.'

They stared at the westering sun which was turning deeper gold as it got lower, already staining the streaky clouds with hints of scarlet.

'I wonder whether the bushrangers have spent our money yet?' Jack wondered.

'Bet they haven't put it in the bank,' Clee commented.

'I want to be rich when I grow up,' Jack said.

'I'm not sure I do. There's better things to have.'

'Like what?'

'Like a mother and father. If you love money too much, you'll end up like old Lovejoy ... with nothing but an owl for a friend.'

'You could have both, couldn't you?' Jack said.

'No. If you're kind to others, you'll never get rich.'

This view troubled Jack. He clearly hoped that it was not the case.

'You know those oranges Luke bought for Lucy? They were a shilling each,' Clee told Jack.

'A shilling!'

'They came from way up north.'

'Bet he wouldn't do that for me,' Jack grumbled.

'Yes, he would. You mean, *you* wouldn't do it for *him*.'

Jack flinched. Clee had become uncomfortably accurate with her observations.

Then suddenly a cart appeared in the distance. It was Lovejoy! They leapt to their feet. Jack paused to arrange some sticks in an arrow pointing in the direction he was heading, then they scampered down the tree.

Clee and Jack crashed through the bush in an effort to intercept the cart. The thick bush which they had been gazing at with such appreciation a few minutes before now clawed at their clothes and whipped into their faces. Jack tripped a couple of times on tangled creeper but got to his feet again quickly. Clee was as sure-footed as a fawn. Jack pulled a face as his leg began to hurt.

They saw the cart-track through the foliage, some distance ahead. Jack held up his hand and they stopped to regain their breath.

Lovejoy appeared in a moment, looking as mean as ever, despite the beauty of the afternoon. He stopped a short way up the track. The youngsters almost panicked, fearing that they had been spotted. But Lovejoy was just checking that the coast was clear. Then he urged his horse down an overgrown and invisible trail.

'Come on,' Jack whispered excitedly.

They were able to shadow Lovejoy quite easily as he could only drive slowly over the uneven ground. He stopped in a small clearing, and in a moment Bones and Ernest rode out from the trees.

It was impossible to get near enough to hear what was being said, but it was obvious what was happening. Lovejoy was selling provisions to the two ruffians. They loaded them on to the pack-horse, completed their transaction and Lovejoy turned his cart around and retraced his steps. The bushrangers rode off slowly, so that the pack-horse could keep up. Jack and Clee looked at each other. Without a word the decision was taken ... They followed the bandits.

*

One of the advantages for Sean of having a job in the main street was that he saw everybody who came and went. He was stacking bags of chaff when he saw a mounted policeman ride up to the watchhouse. It was Sergeant Collins, the officer who had arrested Marcel. Without a moment's hesitation, Sean abandoned his work and darted across the road to see Danks admitting the travel-stained trooper. Sean threw himself to the ground and edged underneath the floorboards. He inched his way over to where he knew Danks' desk was, and turned his ear to listen.

Collins was speaking. 'Our superiors are wondering why you've found out nothing about the bushrangers yet.'

'Well . . . because I'm a very busy man. I'm thinly stretched out here, you know,' Danks blustered.

'Is that so?' Collins queried.

'Oh yes. Did you know that there is a dangerous criminal in Jericho, a man with a record of violence and radicalism?'

'Is there?' Collins didn't sound convinced.

'Luke Greenwood is his name. He's been hanging around with all sorts of riff-raff: Irish rebels, Chinese and other undesirables.'

It wasn't taking Collins long to realize that Danks was a man of prejudices and very doubtful competence.

'Our first job is to track down those bushrangers. Then we can worry about your "dangerous criminal".' Collins humoured the puffed-up bureaucrat.

Sean squeezed silently out from under the floorboards and ran to tell the others. He clambered up the tree and put his head into the tree-hut. He noticed Jack's arrow made of sticks pointing away from town. Just as he was contemplating what to do, Lovejoy's cart rattled into view. Sean scanned the horizon, but there was no sign of his friends.

Clee and Jack trudged up a hill with the scrub still clutching at their clothes. The light was fading and they had to look at the ground more often to be sure of their footing. They had just about reached the end of their tether and Jack was limping badly.

'Looks as though we've lost them,' Clee panted.

'We'll just get to the top of this,' replied Jack.

Clee nodded and they laboured on. They reached the crest of the hill. The valley below had begun to fill with night but they were still able to see their quarry riding up to the wooden hut set into the side of the hill. Jack thumped Clee on the back in triumph. They saw Bones dismount and lead the pack-horse up to the door of the shack. Ernest said something to Bones and then rode off into the trees again.

'Where did Ernest go?' Clee asked.

Jack shrugged, too flushed with success to care. 'We've got them, Clee. That's where all the stuff they've stolen is. We'll be able to get all our money back.'

'Danks will have to believe us now.'

'We'd better go and get him.'

'We'll rest a bit.'

'Why?'

'You should rest your leg, Jack,' Clee said caringly.

'There's nothing wrong with my leg.'

'Why were you limping then?'

'I wasn't,' Jack lied. But he smiled despite himself. It was no use lying to Clee any more. She now knew when he wasn't telling the truth, one of the penalties of getting to know someone very well.

Their happiness was destroyed by the metallic click of a hammer being pulled back on a pistol. They whirled around to stare into Ernest's cruel, twisted face.

'Well, well, well. If it isn't my favourite little brats.'

CHAPTER
EIGHT

Rebecca stirred a pot full of broth, which was bubbling on top of the stove. She was not giving any thought to her job. Her mind was on something else. She heard footsteps and jerked her head up, but it was only Luke.

'No sign of them,' Luke muttered disappointedly.

'Whatever are they up to?'

'It's pretty well dark out there,' Luke told Rebecca.

'They'll turn up soon. They might have gone to Sean's,' said Rebecca, trying to keep her spirits up. She glanced at Lucy who looked a picture of health as she slumbered on. 'She's getting better by the hour,' said Rebecca. Luke nodded. It was as if they were trying to take their minds off their other worry.

There was a scuffle of footsteps again and Luke and Rebecca turned to the door, their faces bright with hope. But it was Sean who entered.

'Come in, Sean, come in.' They were immediately made suspicious by Sean's downcast, sheepish behaviour. 'Have you seen Jack and Clee?'

'Um ... that's what I've come to tell you about ...' Luke and Rebecca cringed at this ominous beginning. 'You see ... we decided to keep a watch on Lovejoy, to see if he could lead us to the bushrangers' hideout ...'

'The bushrangers!' Rebecca gasped. Luke stilled her with his hand and nodded for Sean to continue.

And I think they followed him out towards the Kalangamite Gorge.'

'But why haven't they come back?'

'I'm not sure. Lovejoy's back. Maybe they got lost.

'It can drop below freezing these nights,' Rebecca gasped, horror-stricken.

'They could've found shelter.' Sean tried to soften the blow.

'And maybe they found the bushrangers,' Luke said, his mouth going dry.

It was now pitch black outside and an early mopoke called mournfully for its mate. Rebecca and Luke were beside themselves with anxiety.

Jack and Clee were trussed up like turkeys ready for the oven. They sat back-to-back over by the fire. Bones crocheted quietly, although he was not feeling as content as he usually was; he thought that Ernest had tied the knots too tightly. In fact, he was unhappy that the children were there at all. He thought they should be snug in their own beds at this hour. He had tried to smile reassuringly at Clee once, but Ernest had put a stop to that.

Ernest sat at the table, cleaning and oiling his huge pistol. He seemed to gain great enjoyment from handling this instrument of death. From time to time he glowered at the youngsters. They could not keep their eyes off him, realizing that their fate was being decided in his squinting, mis-shapen mind.

Jack had lost all track of time. He asked Clee whether she

had any idea. Although he whispered, Ernest heard him above the crackle of the fire.

'I thought I told you to keep your mouth shut. Didn't I?' snapped Ernest. Jack just stared, almost hypnotized by Ernest's reptilian eyes. 'Answer me, brat.'

'I suppose ... you did,' Jack quavered.

Ernest reassembled the gun quickly and expertly. He rose with ominous slowness and approached Jack. 'You suppose I did,' he murmured silkily. Jack's heart beat faster and faster with fright. 'You know, I never disliked a kid more than I dislike you. And do you know why?' Jack shrugged. He could not find his voice. 'Do you know why, brat?' Ernest rasped.

'No.' Jack whispered.

'Because you think you're smarter than me, don't you?'

Bones had stopped crocheting, realizing that Ernest had worked himself up into one of his blind fits of rage. 'Ernie ... calm down.'

'Shut up,' snapped Ernest. 'I reckon there's only one way out of this.' He cocked his big pistol and rammed it against Jack's forehead.

'No!' shrieked Clee.

Jack could feel his heart climbing up his chest into his mouth. Ernest started to chuckle madly. He pulled the trigger. There was a click ... the gun wasn't loaded.

Jack blinked and sucked in huge lungfuls of air as if to assure himself he still could. Ernest guffawed. Jack felt the sweat of terror trickling down his back.

Assistant-Commissioner Danks was looking puzzled at what Sean, Rebecca and Luke were saying. Collins sat in the background, listening.

'But why would Mr Lovejoy be going to visit those bush-rangers?'

'Because the children believe they are ... in cahoots together,' Luke explained.

'Fiddlesticks. It's an outrageous suggestion!' Danks turned to Collins. 'This man is trying to blacken Mr Lovejoy's name – and we all know why ... because he knows Mr Lovejoy can denounce him as a criminal! Is that not so?'

Luke sighed with impatience. Young lives were at risk and here they were, wasting time. 'I don't know whether Lovejoy is involved or not. I'm telling you why my children followed him.'

'It's getting very late and we're all tired. Why don't we just go over and see what Mr Lovejoy has to say for himself,' Collins interrupted soothingly.

Jasper stared malevolently at his master's accusers. Love-joy had drawn himself up to his full height and eyed his night visitors haughtily, an air of injured innocence on his face.

'I did go out towards the gorge today to deliver provisions to two miners – that's not a crime, is it?'

'And where do these men live?' Collins inquired.

'I don't know. All prospectors are very cagey about their claims. We met at an arranged spot, miles away from their diggings.'

'That's quite right. Prospectors don't like anybody knowing where they're working,' Danks agreed fawningly.

Collins smiled long-suffering. 'Did you see the Green-wood children today?'

'No, thank goodness.'

'Sean here says they followed your cart,' Collins persisted.

146

'What on earth for?' asked Lovejoy. Sean dropped his eyes. He was tired also and did not feel like explaining their suspicions again.

'Sneaky little devils. They deserve all they get,' Lovejoy barked harshly.

'Two children are missing, man. We are asking your assistance in finding them.' Luke's mild demeanour was starting to wear thin. He had been under a great deal of strain recently with Lucy's illness; now Jack and Clee were lost or, worse, prisoners somewhere in the cold dark night. An ominous fire kindled in his eyes. 'Mr Lovejoy, you can harass me and even my wife as much as you like. We can look after ourselves. But if you or those bushrangers harm just one hair of my son or his friend, I will tear the limbs from your body. You have my word on that. Do you understand me?' Luke's sudden rage took them by surprise. Even Rebecca was taken aback.

Lovejoy and Danks recoiled as if a furnace door had opened. 'You see! He's mad. A crazy anarchist!' Danks gasped.

Collins looked at Luke in a new light. He hadn't taken Danks' allegations seriously, but now he was not so sure. 'We'll start searching at first light,' Collins said.

Lucy sat up in bed. Her angelic face was puckered with worry. Her parents had their heads bowed in prayer. Luke prayed: 'Oh Lord, whose mercy is boundless, please deliver our loved ones, Jack and Cleopatre, from whatever danger they may be in.'

Rebecca and Lucy murmured. 'Amen.'

'And please forgive me for my rage and anger and hate. For it is only love that can achieve anything,' Luke added.

They raised their heads and smiled weakly at one another, trying to banish their worst misgivings. But their eyes could not help returning to the two empty beds ...

The fire was nearly out and the cold was starting to penetrate Jack's limbs. But the chill was a minor discomfort, compared with the fear which gnawed on his mind. Jack had no idea what to do. The ropes were knotted tight and, even if he could free himself, he did not like his chances of getting past Ernest. He tried not to think about what the bandits had in mind for them. The one thing he knew for sure was that he was glad Clee was with him. He looked over towards Ernest and Bones who were lying on rough mattresses. Clee stirred and groaned quietly.

'You cold?' Jack whispered.

'A bit.'

Jack tried to make room for her closer to the fire by cater-pillaring along the floor. 'Is that better?'

'Thanks, Jack. And, Jack, we'll get out of this ... somehow.' Her teeth flashed white as she smiled in reassurance. It was just such a smile that Jack remembered she wore when she was being locked up in the canvas bag and dropped in the barrel of water.

Ernest's voice cut through the dark like a lash. 'Shut up, or I'll shoot you now.'

Clee and Jack tried to shrink back into the darkness. They snuggled closer together to keep the cold and fear at bay. Jack forced a smile, but it curdled and looked more like a grimace.

Sergeant Collins was showing Danks up. It was first light and he was organizing the search parties expertly and without fuss. He instructed Rebecca, Lin, Danks, Doc and four or five diggers how to search without covering the same ground. It was a dismal, cold morning. Even the birds seemed sullen and reluctant to stir. With hearts as leaden as the sky, Rebecca and Luke split up to seek the children.

Luke panted with exertion and impatience as he toiled up a hillside. He paused for a moment to glance back, but soon forged on, realizing he would see more from the top.

Luke had noticed that Jack's hostility towards him seemed to be softening. He was determined that death should not cheat them of the friendship they both longed for.

Luke gained the top of the hill and stared, scanning the panorama again. He groaned in anguish, then, overcome by the futility of his search, he cried out in pain as much as in hope of an answer. 'Jack! Jack! Jack!'

His cry echoed through the valleys and gullies before it trailed away into the vastness of the Australian outback.

Lovejoy stared out of the window of his shop. Sean and Lucy were to be seen, dawdling sadly down the road. Lucy was still weak from her sickness, but she couldn't bear to stay in bed while Jack and Clee were in danger. Lovejoy watched them. It would not be true to say that his conscience was giving him trouble – he had beaten and starved that into submission long ago – but he hoped, a little bit anyway, that no harm would come to Jack and Clee.

He reached into the pocket of his waistcoat and pulled out Lucy's musical locket. He opened it and the haunting nursery-rhyme tune played. His mind flew back to his own childhood, and he remembered a cold nursery with dirty windows set too high to see out of and a procession of thin governesses who taught him never to say what he felt. He knew that, somewhere along the line, he had taken a wrong turn. He had, however. no real wish to mend his ways: and so, the colder and emptier he became. the more precious stones and gold he needed to wink back some light into his gloomy, dusty heart.

He watched the pretty young girl, white-faced from illness. disappear down the street. The spring wound down in her locket and silence descended on Lovejoy. He and Jasper stared at each other, both realizing that they were looking at their only friend. It was difficult to say who was the more disappointed.

Sean and Lucy meandered towards the tree-hut. They passed some diggers who were still fossicking away in their holes. Soon they reached the river and walked along its restful banks.

'Why wouldn't they let us search?' Sean wondered. 'We wouldn't have got lost.'

'I wish there was something we could do,' Lucy nodded.

'I'm glad that policeman's here. Now Danks will have to do something.'

Lucy suddenly stopped, an idea was crystallizing. 'We should get Bojinda.'

'What for?'

'Well, aborigines are good at tracking, aren't they? You know, finding clues.'

'Yes, just what I was thinking myself,' Sean lied as he smiled in congratulation.

They turned and headed off. Suddenly, they got the fright of their lives when they ran straight into Bojinda. But it was a different Bojinda. He had sashes of white paint running across his body and his face was daubed with red ochre. Lucy stifled a scream.

'Quick, we must go quick,' Bojinda said.

'Bojinda, Clee and Jack are lost,' Sean said.

'That is why I come. Quick!'

'How did you know they'd gone missing?' Sean asked.

Bojinda didn't answer, but set off in his effortless lope, balancing his body with his boomerang and spear. Sean and Lucy followed him.

Bojinda stopped now and then to scrutinize the ground or some foliage. Lucy and Sean strained their eyes to see what he was looking at, but whatever clues Bojinda could see were quite invisible to their stupid European eyes.

They soon arrived at the place where the overgrown path led off at a tangent. Bojinda carried on down the main trail. After a short distance, he realized he had gone too far. He straightened and seemed to sniff the breeze like a hound. He gazed around, his brain handling calculations far beyond the grasp of any white man.

'Bojinda, why are you covered in paint?' Lucy wanted to know.

'Bad men ahead. It is a sign for fighting,' Bojinda replied simply.

Bojinda suddenly spotted something. He pointed at some bruised leaves and, peering through the foliage, discovered the hidden path.

Jack jerked awake. He stared around wildly till the horrible truth came clattering back. He tried to ease his cramped limbs and bumped into Clee, who then twitched painfully awake. Her face fell as she remembered too. They were alone now.

'Where are they?' asked Clee.

'They've gone outside.'

Clee tried another fortifying smile, and Jack felt better for it.

'Clee, we're going to have to get out of here. I reckon Ernest is ... mad. Do you reckon you could get out of these ropes?'

Clee looked at her bindings with a professional eye, then commented, 'Father does special knots.' Their spirits were not quite broken – they both managed to smile ruefully at this.

Clee's acrobatic training had made her incredibly supple. She slowly worked at the ropes around her wrists.

A muttered conversation began to leak through the wall.

'It's the only thing we can do,' Ernest was saying.

'I don't mind shooting the odd constable, but ... I couldn't shoot a couple of kids in cold blood,' Bones replied.

Jack and Clee froze in horror, straining their ears.

'A kid's word in court could still put a noose around our necks,' Ernest persisted.

'Let's just leave them here.'

'Listen, Bones, I'm the boss in this outfit. I do the planning. I say we snuff them out.'

Perhaps it was terror that lent Clee strength – one hand, chafed and red, eased out of its bonds.

Bojinda, Sean and Lucy were moving quickly, now that Bojinda had found the horse tracks. Poor Lucy was near exhaustion, not yet fully recovered from her illness. Bojinda, eyes fixed on the ground, climbed the last hill. Suddenly he flung himself down. Sean and Lucy crawled up to join him. He pointed down into the valley. There, clear as daylight, were Bones and Ernest, arguing outside their hut.

'It's them,' Sean muttered excitedly.

'Sean, you go back to get police. I will light fire down there to make smoke.'

Without another word, Sean leapt to his feet and was off like a hare. Lucy touched Bojinda on the arm and smiled. They watched the bandits go back into the hideout and wondered what fate Jack and Clee might have met.

Clee had finished untying her knots and was now free. They heard the heavy tread of their captors.

Jack had a brainwave. 'Clee, throw your voice,' he whispered.

Clee frowned, not sure whether she had heard him correctly.

'Throw your voice,' Jack repeated.

Ernest shambled over, wearing a threadbare expression of friendliness.

'Listen, we want to take you for a little walk in the bush,' he lilted evilly.

'This must be the hideout. Let's get the police!' a girl's voice seemed to say from just outside.

Bones and Ernest swung round. They were astonished. Hadn't they just come from outside? And that voice, it sounded like Clee.

Ernest gawped at Clee's unmoving lips as the voice was heard to call again, 'Let's get out of here before they come back.'

Ernest and Bones sprinted outside. In a moment, Clee

wriggled out of her loosened bonds. Jack grinned in congratulation. She bent down to untie him.

'Don't! Scram! Get help!' But Clee ignored Jack and continued to work away at the ropes. Then they heard the bushrangers coming back. Clee glanced around desperately, then jumped up and hid herself behind the door.

If the two bandits had been bewildered before, now they looked absolutely flabbergasted: Clee had vanished, leaving a neat pile of rope on the floor. They stood there, gaping.

'Where is she?' Ernest gasped. He advanced threateningly on Jack. In a flash, Clee sprang out from behind the door and raced off. Bones and Ernest swung around and gave chase.

As Clee darted in and out of the trees, the circulation flooded back into her limbs, with rushes of pins-and-needles. Bones was an ungainly mover, his thin legs knocking into each other as he ran. But Ernest was more agile. He was narrowing the gap. Clee ducked and weaved. Ernest made a snatch at her streaming hair and it was only by ducking at the last moment that she was saved.

Suddenly a spear was thrust out from behind a tree in between Ernest's scampering legs. He was utterly skittled. He lay there, stunned and confused. Bojinda darted out and retrieved his spear. Ernest scowled. He was furious. He would have liked to cut Bojinda's heart out there and then, but he couldn't move.

Lucy appeared and grabbed Clee's hand, and then they both vanished into the bush again. Then Bones arrived and looked down sympathetically at Ernest. Ernest suspected that Bones didn't really want to catch Clee, but there was no time to accuse him of that just then. He got up on one elbow and unholstered his pistol.

'I'll kill them all!' he gasped, as he struggled to his feet.

Lucy and Clee soon discovered that they had run into a steep-sided gully. They forced their way deeper and deeper through the tangled vegetation, to find that the only way out was upwards, and this would expose them to gunfire.

They heard Ernest come wheezing up and stop, some twenty paces away. He knew they were close by but he couldn't see them. With a sneer of cruelty he raised his gun and continued to stalk the girls. Suddenly, there was an odd whistling noise as Bojinda's boomerang sliced through the air. Ernest screamed as it whacked the pistol out of his hand. The gun fell to the ground and went off. Bojinda appeared on the cliff above the girls and pulled them to safety, as Ernest's screams of pain echoed through the gully.

Sean was completely puffed out, but he plodded gamely back to Jericho for help. In the distance, he saw two familiar figures. As they approached, he recognized them.

'Mr Greenwood! Mr Greenwood! Hey!'

Luke and Rebecca broke into a run.

'Sean, any news?' Luke demanded, grabbing him by the shoulders.

'We've found them. They're in a little valley just past Kalangamite Gorge,' Sean panted.

'Are they all right?' Rebecca asked.

'The bushrangers have got them,' Sean said gloomily.

Rebecca and Luke gasped. 'Rebecca, go back and fetch the police,' Luke said quickly.

'Bojinda's making a fire. Just tell them to follow the smoke.' Sean told Rebecca. Rebecca nodded. They set off in opposite directions.

'Luke, be careful!' Rebecca cried as she started to run back to Jericho.

Despite all his efforts, Jack had not managed to loosen the knots – he was awaiting the return of his tormentors with dread, burning to know whether Clee had escaped.

The bandits re-entered the hut. Ernest's right hand hung, useless, by his side. It was beginning to swell. He was in a filthy mood, shouting and jabbering.

He grabbed Jack by the throat and hauled him up to face level. 'Listen, brat, your nigger mate out there damn near broke my wrist. I was a happy man until you came along. Now you've just about ruined everything, so you're going to pay.'

Bones was feverishly sorting the booty they had accumulated. 'Come on, Ernie. They're bound to raise the alarm in Jericho.'

Ernest let Jack go and he fell to the floor in a heap. Then Ernest lifted a big leather bag on to the table and started sorting and throwing valuables into it, still addressing Jack. 'And listen. There's no need to rejoice. Because when we leave here we're going to burn all this evidence, and you're part of it. So, unfortunately, you're going to go up in smoke, too. Isn't that a shame?' Ernest finished with mock-sadness.

Bones was about to toss Luke's chamois pouch full of guineas into his sack when Ernest snatched it from him and stowed it in his. 'I'll take the money and jewellery,' Ernest barked.

'Hang on, Ernie. How come?'

'It doesn't matter who takes it. We're going to be together,' Ernest explained.

'What if we get split up?'

'We'll meet up afterwards.'

Ernest had bullied and brow-beaten Bones once too often. Bones grabbed a handful of jewellery and a purse that clinked promisingly and put them in his bag. 'So it doesn't matter who takes what, does it?'

Ernest accidentally banged his own swollen hand, and his rage returned. 'Listen, what's got into you? We're partners, aren't we? We share.'

'Seems to me that that means you take what you want and I get the left-overs.'

Suddenly, their argument was interrupted by the arrival of Luke. He burst in through the door, trying to adjust his eyes to the gloom. He scanned the room for Jack.

'Jack!'

But Ernest had quick reflexes. He held his pistol in his left hand trained unwaveringly on Luke.

'Move, and you're a dead man.'

Luke halted. His heart went out to his son, shivering and sick with fear. Luke started to measure distances, calculate possibilities. His body, for so many years at peace, now tensed for battle once more.

'Get out! They'll shoot you!' Jack gabbled, his voice cracking with hysteria.

Suddenly, Luke looked different. He looked dangerous, threatening. His eyes shone and the air seemed to crackle with danger. He said, 'I've just come to take my son home.'

'And squeal to the police,' Ernest rasped.

'They're already coming. It's all over,' Luke said.

'For you, it is.'

'Just let me take him and go.' Luke was inching towards his son.

Ernest turned the gun towards Jack. 'Stay still or your brat cops it!'

Jack was exhausted and half mad with terror. The muzzle of the gun pointing at his chest finally broke the last strands of his control. Jack felt a ripping in his head. 'Don't ... Dad ... Dad ... Please don't let them hurt me.'

Jack had managed to loosen his ropes just enough to stand. He stumbled towards Luke.

Nothing on earth could have stopped Luke from rushing to catch him. He had now placed his body between the gun and Jack.

Ernest's face was set with murderous resolve.

Luke embraced Jack, who clung to him, sobbing. Luke's mind was too full to think about the bullet which at any moment might thud into his back.

Bones watched the father and son hug each other fiercely. As Ernest squeezed the trigger, Bones knocked the gun up. The slug passed harmlessly into the roof.

Ernest stared uncomprehendingly at his partner. 'What! You fool ...' Ernest scrabbled in his belt for another bullet, but Bones clouted him on his damaged wrist. The gun fell to the floor with a thud. 'I'll get you for this,' Ernest screamed.

The quiet, reasonable voice of Sergeant Collins cut through the gunpowder-heavy air: 'Leave the gun where it is and put your hands where I can see them!'

Collins walked into the room with his service revolver drawn. Ernest scowled and nursed his wrist. He knew he was beaten.

Luke held Jack tenderly as the boy shook with weeping.

The sound that echoed in Luke's ear was not the crack of the pistol, though that had been deafening in the confined space, but Jack's cry of 'Dad! Dad!' which seemed to have come from the very bottom of his heart. Both had escaped with more than their lives. They now had each other.

Even if the oil-lamps were not alight, the Greenwoods' tent would have glowed in the soft spring night, so full of joy was it.

Collins dropped Luke's money pouch on the table. 'It's obviously your money, Sir. I'm glad you got it back.'

'Thank you, Sergeant,' Luke said with feeling. Rebecca smiled her appreciation too.

Collins turned to the children and frowned in mock-sternness. 'And next time, leave it to the people whose job it is to catch the law-breakers, will you?'

'We'd have to wait till doomsday for Danks to do anything,' Sean retorted.

'Don't be cheeky. Sean. Sergeant Collins is right,' Luke rebuked him.

'What's going to happen to Mr Lovejoy?' Jack inquired.

'Well, nothing. He hasn't broken any law that we know of.'

'But he's in cahoots with the bushrangers,' Clee said.

'They deny that he is. Said he just brought them their provisions,' Collins informed them.

'So there *is* honour amongst thieves, after all,' Rebecca observed.

'We don't know that he is a thief, Ma'am.'

'The Sergeant is right, a man is innocent until proven guilty.' Luke had become the mild-mannered family man again.

'What's going to happen to the bushrangers, Sir?' Clee asked.

'They'll be taken back to Melbourne to stand trial.' Collins rose and moved to the door, putting on his cap. He turned and looked indulgently at the youngsters. 'While I cannot officially approve of you taking the law into your own hands, I think you were very brave. We've got a lot to thank you for.'

All the children beamed.

'One last thing, Sergeant,' said Luke. 'Do you remember an arrest you made some months back? A Frenchman by the name of ...'

'Marcel Duberau,' Collins interrupted him. 'My head's still spinning after being with him ... I've never met a prisoner who had so much to say for himself.'

'I wonder if you could take some money back to discharge his debts.' Luke turned to Clee. 'How much does he owe now, Clee?'

Clee smiled like a sunrise. She jumped up and embraced Luke. Jack looked on approvingly. He was enjoying being a part of the emotional circle which he had shunned for so long.

The Greenwoods stood watching as Danks led the bushrangers out of Jericho. Their hands were shackled and their horses were roped together. Danks gave the youngsters a dirty look and sniffed archly. The Greenwoods walked along beside Bones' horse.

'Thank you for what you did. I've asked to speak at your trial to tell the judge of your action,' Luke said to the bushranger.

'That's good of you, Sir.' Bones smiled shyly.

'Is there anything I can do for you?' Luke asked.

'Ah ...' Bones began sheepishly. 'I would appreciate it if you could send me some ... wool in prison.'

'Some wool!'

'I like to crochet. It takes my mind off things. It's very restful, you know.'

'Why, yes, of course. I'll send it by the next coach.'

'He's a good lad, that one,' Bones said, nodding at Jack. 'Didn't want him getting killed. Goodbye.'

Everybody was quite moved by the gangly, unpleasant-looking fellow and bade him farewell warmly.

Ernest rode past, leaned down, and hissed at Jack poisonously. 'Don't close both eyes when you sleep, brat. I'll be back with my knife to settle up with you.'

Collins rode up quickly and jostled Ernest aside. Then he saluted and said, 'Goodbye. And try to give Officer Danks a hand when he gets back. His heart's in the right place.'

The Greenwoods smiled and waved. Other diggers were also watching the cavalcade make its way out of town.

Rebecca put her arms around Clee and Lucy. Luke put his arm around Jack's shoulders, hesitantly. Jack did not freeze and flinch as he used to, but looked up and smiled.

Later that day, Jack sat on his bed in the tent hot with the midday sun, his head full of thoughts. His eyes travelled up to the 'BLESS THIS HOUSE' plaque. It had never been the same since Ernest took to it. He reached up and lifted it down, and inspected the damage: the frame was twisted and broken.

161

Rebecca entered and looked fondly at him for a moment. 'Are you all right, Jack?'

Jack looked up and nodded as his mother came and sat on the bed next to him.

'The others are wondering where you are. They want to play.'

'I don't feel like it.'

'Is your leg hurting?'

Jack shook his head. He looked down at the plaque. 'Father gave me this the same week he caught the fever.'

'Ah, is that what the trouble is?' Rebecca thought she understood.

'No ...'

Rebecca did not follow. She looked at Jack quizzically.

'I just feel strange about Luke ...' Jack stammered. 'The way I've been to him. The things I've done and said.'

'But there's been a reason for it, Jack. Luke understands that.'

'Does he?'

'Of course. He knew that you didn't want to forget your first father.'

'I thought Luke was scared. A coward. But he's not. Ernest was going to shoot him and Luke wasn't scared at all.'

'He *was* scared. We're all very scared inside. But he would've faced a hundred guns to rescue you ... to do what he thought was right.'

'Would he?'

'He loves you more than his own life, Jack.'

Jack's eyes dropped to the plaque, and he thought about this. He looked at his mother again, and she nodded to reinforce her statement.

162

'It's funny. this place,' Jack muttered. 'It makes you forget lots of things.'

'We never forget completely, Jack. Our hearts are big enough to hold everything we put in them. But it's not good to brood on things. either. Remembering doesn't have to be brooding.'

Jack toyed with the plaque as this sank in. He pulled off a broken piece. 'It's broken.'

'It can be fixed. Luke'll make some glue for it. He's good at mending things.'

Jack nodded, but he was still confused by the old and new thoughts jostling in his mind.

Rebecca put her arms around him and gave him a big hug. 'Everything'll be all right. Jack. It always is in the end. You'll see.'

Rebecca would not have been so confident if she had known who was travelling towards Jericho by coach at that moment. One of the passengers would have delighted her: Marcel, still pale and shorn from prison, was staring delightedly out at the early summer countryside. Even above the jingling of harnesses, the commotion of the birds and bees and bugs and beetles could be heard. Marcel was jealously protecting a bunch of flowers on his lap from the pitching and tossing of the carriage.

The identity of the other passenger, however, would have made Rebecca's blood run cold.

'My name is Sugden. I am a circuit magistrate,' the man introduced himself.

Marcel recoiled in horror. 'A magistrate. I have come straight out of prison into the clutches of another judge.'

'Prison, Sir?'

'A small misunderstanding over a debt. Which is completely paid, I'm glad to say. Thanks to the generosity of a friend.'

'I'm pleased to hear that,' Sugden boomed disapprovingly.

'I am returning to Jericho to thank my friend for his *largesse*.'

'I'm afraid the purpose of my visit is not so pleasant. I have to fine a lot of wretched miners for not paying their licence fees. I also must bring to justice an arsonist and would-be murderer, who fled here from Dudley in England.'

'Truly?'

'Masquerading as a family man and prospector, hoping to escape detection. Thankfully someone has recognized him and informed the authorities. It's up to me to deal with him now.'

Marcel raised his eyebrows in polite interest. He would have paid much greater attention to the magistrate's story if he had known whom he was referring to, but he allowed his eyes to stray out of the window again. After the greystone walls of gaol, the infinite blue heavens and the endless green bush were a sight for sore eyes.

CHAPTER
NINE

Marcel felt as sunny inside as the day was outside, at the thought of seeing Clee again. He looked down at the bunch of flowers, little enough thanks to the Greenwoods. When he started performing again he would repay them properly. He looked out of the swaying window again. They had crested a hill and were descending into an enormous valley.

He turned to the magistrate. 'This country. you know, it is so ... huge and empty as though the horizon is further away than in Europe.'

'It's because there are no marks of man's presence here,' Sugden commented.

'You are right. No haystacks, no barns, no church steeples,' Marcel agreed.

'All that will change as more people come from the old country.'

Marcel shot a troubled look at Sugden. He had managed to keep his political views to himself for the long journey – he could no longer. 'I like it the way it is, with the space ... when man is so small, as he should be.'

'But, dear Sir, you must admit, it has its drawbacks. For example, it is hard to impose British law on such a far-flung and tiny population.'

'What a lucky escape for them! They have no need for British law.'

'It is statements like that, Sir, that have led to outbreaks of lawlessness on the goldfields,' Sugden snapped.

'And I say good to that. This is Australia, Monsieur. Your Latin will tell you, that means "southern". Forgive me for reminding you that England is in the northern hemisphere.'

'And France, too.'

'*Mais oui*, and content to stay there. This must be a new country. Do not bring old mistakes here.'

'The Queen's rule is not a mistake, Sir.'

The driver had stopped to water the horses, and his passengers' voices suddenly seemed very loud. A horse whinnied and stamped. The driver clicked his tongue as the voices rose to a shout.

'If her law is so precious, let her keep it close by her side in London.'

'Let me remind you, Sir, that none of the excesses of your revolution have contaminated the shores of England.'

The nervous horse stamped again. The driver had had enough. 'Hey, you in there ... Gentlemen. All that shouting is frightening the horses.'

There was golden silence for a moment, then Marcel started again. 'And what benefits does Australia receive from being the unfortunate victim of Britain's kindness?'

The driver spat a jet of tobacco juice over the side of the coach. 'Politics!'

The Greenwoods sat around the rough table, holding a family conference. Luke and Jack sat next to each other. Lucy could hardly believe that her dearest wish had come true.

'As you know, we came to the goldfields to seek our fortune,' Luke began. 'I'm afraid I was a dismal failure at that. Now that we've had our money returned, we can go back to Melbourne if we wish. So tell me, do you want to stay here or go back to the city?'

Without hesitation, Jack gave his vote: 'Stay!'

'I don't want to go back. All our friends are here now,' agreed Lucy.

'Your father and I intend to buy a couple of cows. We hope that selling fresh milk and bread will give us a living,' Rebecca said.

'What about Lovejoy?' Jack asked.

'Somehow I think Mr Lovejoy has learnt his lesson.' Luke looked steadily at Jack. Jack didn't know how much Luke had learnt about his sabotage. Jack couldn't help smiling, and Luke smiled back.

There was a cheerful knock on the doorpost and Marcel burst in with all the flair of a showman.

'*Bonjour! C'est moi!* Hello, *mes amis!*'

'Papa!' Clee was on her feet and in his arms in an instant. The others rose and crowded around.

Marcel hugged his daughter while trying to protect the bouquet of flowers. 'Careful, *ma petite.* You look well.'

'It's so good to see you, Papa.'

Marcel gave the flowers to Rebecca. 'Madame, for you.'

'I'm glad everything went as arranged,' Luke said.

Marcel shook his hand warmly. 'Monsieur, how can I ever repay you?'

'It's a gift. I do not expect anything in return.'

'Luke, I am convinced that the Battle of Waterloo was a mistake. With friendship like ours, what need was there of the Hundred Years War between our countries?

Luke and Rebecca laughed at this extravagant performer.

Marcel hugged his daughter again, then turned to Jack and Lucy. 'And you two, I hope you looked after my little girl for me. Did you?'

'We tried.'

'Actually, she looked after us.'

Marcel cocked an eyebrow.

'She helped save me from the bushrangers.'

'Bushrangers! What is this?'

'It's a long story, Papa.'

Marcel sat down and lifted Clee on to his lap. 'Tell me, tell me all of it – and do not leave out a thing, not a single heartbeat.'

'Well, it all started when Jack saw Mr Lovejoy with Luke's wallet . . .' Clee began.

'No! Start from the beginning,' interrupted Jack. 'The beginning was when we were robbed.'

'That's not the beginning,' piped up Lucy.

'Looks like it'll be a long evening, Marcel,' Luke commented over the squabbling. But nobody would have had it any other way.

Danks sat with an expression of great deference on his face across the desk from Magistrate Sugden. Sugden had a large pile of charges before him which he was working through.

'And what about Luke Greenwood, Your Honour?' Danks asked eagerly.

Sugden reached into his case and took out an official-looking document. 'It would probably be more appropriate if you left that form of address until the court proceedings.'

'Oh yes, Sir, I'm so sorry.'

'Your information was correct. A Luke David Greenwood spent seven years in gaol for incitement to riot and malicious wounding.'

'I thought so. I knew. A thoroughly nasty piece of work.'

'The prison authorities remembered him quite well. Seems he was a model prisoner.'

'Wolf in sheep's clothing . . . which is exactly what his trick is here. Devoted family man, huh!'

'I take it you don't like the man,' Sugden probed, looking at Danks askance.

'He's a trouble-maker, Sir. It's types like him who start problems . . . like the Eureka incident.'

'I want you to warn him not to leave Jericho.'

'Why not throw him in prison now, Sir?'

'I'm sitting at Creswick tomorrow.'

'But shouldn't he be under lock and key?'

'He hasn't been tried yet, Mr Danks. Now if you'll excuse me . . .' He indicated that he wanted to return to the paper-work.

'Yes, of course, Your Honour. I'm sorry, Your Honour. I mean Sir . . . Sir,' Danks stammered.

'That will be all, Danks.'

Bojinda sat motionless in the tree-hut. He had been expecting his friends all morning. For a people who measure their history, not in centuries, but in millennia, a few hours' wait was nothing. In fact, Bojinda had stepped into the dreaming. He had been dreaming a lot lately in order to make some sense of what was happening to his people. The Europeans had just murdered three of his tribe for stealing a sheep; and his cousin had told him that, further north, there were massacres on an even bigger scale.

According to the aborigines, the dreaming was not just the past, but an invisible part of the present which ran parallel to their ordinary waking life. It flowed like a river from the past into the future and was made up of the dreaming, all the wisdom and experience, of his ancestors and of his descendants also.

Bojinda had some sad news for the others. His tribe had decided to move into the interior, further away from the bloodthirsty clayfaces. He would be sorry to lose his good friends and he hoped they would not grow up to be like the yelling men with smoking guns who rode through his people's camp sites, leaving behind grief and loathing.

Bojinda had tried to explain what the dreamtime was, but the English language had no words rich enough to describe it, and none of them had really understood, except perhaps Lucy. But then Lucy and Bojinda didn't need words to understand each other. She was too young to have built the walls of words and thinking which do not exist in the heart of either black or white, or in the dreaming.

He heard laughing and shouting down below, and soon his friends were poking their heads over the wooden platform.

'Bojinda's here,' Jack shouted delightedly. Lucy was the first to notice that Bojinda was wearing a new leather belt. She had seen them in Lovejoy's shop. They were fancily tooled but rather ugly, Lucy thought.

'Where'd you get the belt from?' Lucy asked.

'Ted. I give one of these.' Bojinda pointed to his wombat-skin jacket.

'That was too much,' Jack commented.

'It was old and torn.' Bojinda grinned. They were all glad that Ted hadn't got the best of the bargain.

'Where did Ted get the belt?' asked Jack.

'He say he found it,' Bojinda replied.

'He's never got any money. Stole it, more like,' said Sean. Everybody nodded.

'Clee's going back to Melbourne soon,' Lucy told Bojinda.

'My dad's come back,' Clee explained. 'We've got to get back on the road to make a living. Be good to have a rest, too. It's been pretty hectic here.'

Everybody laughed.

Then Bojinda spoke. 'I too going away.'

The others were upset and expressed their disappointment loudly.

'My people had a meeting. There are too many clayfaces coming. We no longer live in the way that is good.' Bojinda frowned as he uttered these painful words. His listeners went quiet. 'Also the men who have sheep . . . yesterday they shoot some of my tribe.'

'No!' Lucy frowned.

'They can't do that!'

Bojinda interrupted the chorus of outrage. 'It is best that we go far away.' They all subsided into an unhappy silence, stealing looks at Bojinda from time to time. But his face was impassive, as it always was when he was not smiling. He stared sightlessly into infinity. They all realized as if by intuition that the problem would never have an easy answer.

Bojinda stirred and undid the two necklaces of dried seeds threaded on plaited dingo hair from around his neck. He solemnly slipped first one around Lucy's neck and then the

171

other around Clee's. The girls were very touched and awed because of the gravity with which Bojinda bestowed them.

'I will stay until Clee leaves. You have been good friends – we must always remember. No matter what happens.'

The tree-hut usually resounded with laughter, insults, boasting and jokes, but now it was completely still. They all realized that something was over. Bojinda would walk out of their lives, perhaps for ever. Clee too would depart to take up her fairground calling. They had been driven together for a time and now they were being driven apart once again. The river flowed under their feet and the wind sighed through the leaves. They looked at one another, every detail stencilling itself on to their minds.

Sugden had become so irritated with Danks' fawning manners and his enthusiasm for flogging and hanging, that he had kept him outside the office. Danks consoled himself by strutting up and down the street, glowering at the diggers.

Suddenly, he heard a man shouting. 'I've been robbed! I've been robbed!' Lovejoy bellowed at him from across the street. 'Officer Danks. A crime. Over here, quickly.'

So great was the alarm Lovejoy was raising that passers-by were quite convinced his whole stock had been stolen.

Danks wheezed up. 'I have lost two belts. They were on a rack by the door. It's disgraceful!' shouted Lovejoy.

'Something will have to be done about this,' Danks muttered ineffectually.

'Still, since international criminals are allowed to roam the streets at will, I don't suppose anything's safe.' Lovejoy suddenly squinted at something over Danks' shoulder. 'There's the culprit!'

He descended the steps and flapped off down the street like a scrawny vulture. The youngsters watching him really believed that he had finally gone mad. He scuttled towards them, all arms, legs and rage.

'Thief! You black-hearted scoundrel!' He grabbed hold of the belt around Bojinda's waist and tried to wrench it off. The others milled around, trying to make him stop by dragging on his clothing and yelling at him.

Bojinda seemed quite aloof from the free-for-all. He made no attempt to protect himself and looked straight through Lovejoy.

'Give it back, thief,' Lovejoy squawked. He finally unbuckled the belt and held on to it as if it were studded with diamonds.

'You're the thief!' Jack exploded.

Danks arrived, heaving and puffing.

'Where did you get that belt from, boy?'

'It's mine,' Bojinda replied.

'Listen, try to make it easy for yourself. Tell me where you got it from,' Danks boomed threateningly.

Bojinda stared back impassively. The white youngsters couldn't understand why Bojinda made no attempt to clear his name.

'Tell them,' prompted Lucy. But Bojinda held his peace. Danks was beginning to wilt as the aborigine's black, unseeing eyes drilled through him.

Sean and Jack were reluctant to inform on Ted, but Lucy's loyalties were clearer-cut. 'It was Ted Thomas who took the belt,' she blurted out.

'Is that who you got it from, son?' Danks demanded.

Bojinda still made no reply.

'Oh, arrest him. These black fellas have no idea of private property.' urged Lovejoy.

'You better come with me, Danks said. taking Bojinda by the arm.

The youngsters pursued him like angry hornets. 'He didn't do it.'

'Lovejoy's got it back anyway.' Jack shouted.

Passers-by turned and gaped at the noisy procession as it moved towards the watchhouse. Lovejoy looked down at the belt and noticed that it was scratched. 'Prison's too good for them,' he muttered as he made his way back towards his shop.

Danks snapped the manacles around Bojinda's wrists.

'Mr Danks, don't you understand? He didn't steal it.' said Lucy.

'Ted did,' came a voice.

'Clear off or I'll have to fetch your parents.' Danks held his hand up for silence.

'Hello,' came the voice again. 'Anyone at home?' Jack had to smile. It was Clee's voice, but her lips did not move.

Danks moved off towards the watchhouse. 'And I don't want to find you kids here when I come back.'

'Well, that's got rid of him,' Clee said with satisfaction.

'I *thought* it was you,' Jack applauded.

'Bojinda, please tell them who really did it,' Lucy pleaded. But Bojinda remained silent and inscrutable; he had turned mute because his honour had been insulted.

'We've got to find Ted,' Lucy cried desperately.

Ted was fishing on the riverbank. He was sitting on Bojinda's old wombat-skin jacket and wearing the other stolen belt. He was feeling very happy. Things had become a lot easier around Jericho, now that peace had been declared between his gang and Sean's crowd ... in fact, it had given him time to reflect on who their real enemy was. Accordingly, he had done something to decrease Mr Lovejoy's astronomical profits. It had not been easy, mind you, with the shopkeeper and his eerie bird watching so closely.

Ted's happiness came to an abrupt end when Jack, Clee, Lucy and Sean descended on him.

'Ted, Bojinda's been locked up for stealing that belt,' Sean shouted.

'You've got to own up, Ted.'

'Now hang on,' Ted began.

'Please!' implored Lucy. Ted stared at his fishing-pole, not at all attracted by the idea.

'Otherwise Bojinda will really cop it,' Clee declared.

'Danks doesn't like aborigines,' Lucy said.

'I didn't get caught,' Ted replied.

'He'll die if they lock him up,' Lucy said tearfully.

'We'll stand by you, Ted,' Sean urged.

Ted weighed up the pros and cons. Owning up was as unnatural to him as a fish gobbling down a hook with no bait on it.

'You're not scared are you, Ted?' Jack goaded him shrewdly. Ted glared at Jack.

Sugden flung open the watchhouse door and collapsed into Danks' chair. He was weary and dirty on his return from Creswick.

'The roads out here are getting worse, not better.'

'It's the heavy rain that does it, Sir,' Danks observed solemnly.

Sugden was amazed at Danks' genius for stating the obvious. 'I know that, man. This country will be the death of me.'

'Sir, another case has come up.'

'Something a little more interesting than miners' licences, I hope.'

'I think so, Sir. One of the natives has stolen a belt from Mr Lovejoy's store.'

'A belt!'

'Yes, Sir.'

'A belt, Danks?' Sugden snapped.

'Er . . . yes . . . For holding up trousers.'

'I know what they're for. How much is this belt worth?'

Eager to show his professional competence, Danks whipped his notebook out. 'A shilling.' Danks was beginning to sweat under Sugden's exasperated scrutiny. 'Or . . . er . . . one shilling and one penny, depending on how much, er . . . you sell it for.'

'Mr Danks, I didn't come a hundred miles over one of the worst roads in the world to preside over tupenny-ha'penny cases.'

Danks was saved from any further criticism by a timid knock at the door, and Ted entered.

'Can't you see I'm busy, boy,' Danks barked.

Ted stared at the men, trying to pluck up courage to confess. 'It wasn't Bojinda who took the belts. It was me, Sir,' Ted gabbled bravely.

'Ah-ha! Now we are getting somewhere,' trumpeted Danks.

'Assistant-Commissioner, restore the belts to their rightful owner. Let both youths go, the innocent one as well. Then come back and help me with the cases for tomorrow,' Sugden spoke icily.

Ted began to smile with relief, until Danks shot him a look that would open a dozen oysters.

Danks was still smarting when he marched down to the Greenwoods' claim. He vented his anger on Luke: 'Are you Luke David Greenwood?'

'Of course I am. You know that.'

'Please accompany me to the watchhouse where you will be formally charged with giving false information to an officer of the crown. Follow me!'

Luke had been expecting this. He hurled the spade into the bank and rubbed the clay off his hands disgustedly.

As soon as Rebecca and the children had heard what had happened, they rushed to the watchhouse but were turned away. Luke would be held in custody until the trial the next day. When they got home, Jack insisted that his mother tell him the full story. As Rebecca related some of Luke's background, Jack's eyes grew wider and wider.

'When Luke was back in England, long before I ever knew him, the owners of the potteries there decided to reduce all the workers' wages by sevenpence a week. But the workers could not afford to live on less money than they already earned. So they went out on to the streets to show their anger. Luke joined a band of men who put the boilers in the pottery works out of action. One night, troops were called out … They fired their carbines into the crowd. Luke snatched a gun from the nearest trooper, smashed it and threw it back. Four other soldiers grabbed him. It needed that many because Luke was very angry. After that, he was put in prison for seven years.'

Jack could hardly believe his ears. The man he had looked down on for being so meek and mild was a violent fire-brand, ready to lay down his life for a cause.

'Why ... why ... didn't he tell me about this?'

'He didn't want you to know. He wants to forget it for ever. That's why he came to Australia, to start again.'

'I think Australia is good for starting again.' Lucy said matter-of-factly.

Jack realized that he had to start again, too. However, his new start did not require a change of country, but a change of heart.

Justice was dispensed in the open air in Jericho. Sugden sat on the verandah of the watchhouse behind Danks' desk, which had been moved out for the occasion. Danks stood next to him. Sugden had a pile of charges in front of him. Sugden had just fined a miner five pounds for not possessing a miner's licence. The circuit magistrate was not a very popular figure on the goldfields and the diggers heckled and jeered at him.

Sugden pulled the next case-sheet towards him. 'Would Luke David Greenwood stand before the bench.'

Rebecca squeezed his arm as Luke stepped forward. Clee, Jack, Lucy and Sean stood, looking strained and worried. Marcel stood next to Rebecca, an expression of righteous anger on his face.

'You are charged that on the tenth day of June, 1853, you did supply false information to a properly constituted officer

178

of the crown, namely Assistant-Commissioner Danks. How do you plead?'

'Guilty.' Luke swallowed. There was a murmur of sympathy from the assembled diggers. Rebecca closed her eyes. Marcel took her arm consolingly. The children felt sick at heart. Things looked very bad.

Sugden turned to Danks who made a big show of consulting his notebook.

'Thank you, Your Honour. When the accused arrived in Jericho, Mr Uriah Lovejoy recognized him immediately and informed me. When the accused applied for a miner's licence I asked him whether he had ever been in gaol, and he denied it. I asked him to swear this on oath but he declined. Since then, he has habitually consorted with unsavoury elements . . .'

'Whom do you mean precisely?' Sugden inquired.

'Er . . . the people who are not . . . of law-abiding nature or of English stock . . . like the Chinese, the Irish and others.'

Sugden realized he was dealing with a nincompoop.

'And he has given vent to radical and anarchist opinions,' Danks continued.

Doc Slope could stand it no longer. He stepped forward abruptly, waving his silver-topped cane. 'Hogwash and hokum. That man is the most law-abiding citizen it has ever been my pleasure to meet in my rich and varied existence.'

'Order! Order! Order!' Sugden beat his gavel.

'Order yourself, Your Eminence! We all had to listen to the lies spouted by that puddin'-head and we were as nice as pie now it's our turn.'

For a moment Sugden was daunted by this outlandish

179

figure and his fruity. Dixie accent. but then he recovered. 'Sir. unless you desist. I will have you arrested for contempt of court!

'All right. I just want to say that this fine country here needs more men like Luke Greenwood and fewer men like that parasite. Uriah Lovejoy.'

All the diggers acclaimed this statement with clapping and cheering.

'Has the accused anything to say?'

Luke spoke with quiet dignity. 'It is true that I lied to Officer Danks. But I had to find gold so that my family would not starve. I am heartily sorry for this falsehood, but I could see no other course of action.' His friends and family looked at him with anxious affection. The diggers nodded their heads at the truth of what he said. 'I spent seven long years in prison for what I did in England. It was there I resolved never to raise my hand in anger again, and nor have I to this day.'

'Do we have a witness to attest to what Mr Greenwood declares?' Sugden called.

'Do you think I was just whistling "Dixie", Your Worship?' Doc bellowed.

Marcel shouldered his way forward. 'I, Marcel Duberau, must speak.'

'Do you know the accused?' Sugden asked long-sufferingly.

'Like my own brother. Monsieur Greenwood is kind to others and good to his family. In France, such a man is not put in prison, but asked to serve in public office. But France is a republic, where such sensible things must happen. In France ...'

'Silence. Step down,' Sugden shouted.

'*Liberté, égalité, fraternité!*' Marcel shouted.

'This is an English court, Sir, and if you utter another word of that language, I will have you arrested. Is there anyone else who can stick to the facts more successfully?'

Jack suddenly found himself stepping forward. 'Me, Sir.'

'And who are you, young man?'

'My name is Jack Greenwood,' Jack declared in proud, ringing tones.

'This boy is a hopeless liar, Your Honour.' Danks jumped in quickly.

'Pray continue, Master Greenwood,' invited Sugden, ignoring Danks.

Luke's heart swelled with pride as Jack owned his surname for the first time.

Jack swallowed. 'Since we came here, things have not been all that good. Some people have been nasty to us, even wrecked our place. A lot of times I wanted to fight back or even get a gun, but he, my father, would not let me.' Luke stood accused of a crime for which he could be sent to prison, but even this threat could not dull the pride he felt at Jack's words. And Jack went on. 'My father would not get angry. He said that the law would find out who had done the evil deeds and punish them. He is not a violent man ... In fact, he is the best father anybody could have.'

The diggers erupted. 'Let him go!' ... 'What's he done wrong?' ... 'Are you stupid as well as greedy?' they screamed.

Jack went back to his place, to be hugged by the women and thumped on the back by Sean, as the diggers' shouts echoed in their ears.

'Order! Silence! Be quiet!' Sugden banged the gavel as hard as he could until the noise died down. 'The charge against the accused is not a minor one. I could, if I wished, bring down the full weight of the law on him, but I do not think it would accord with the true spirit of British justice here. Luke Greenwood, what you have done you have done out of compassion, not for any criminal purpose. Case dismissed.'

Luke's family and friends were overjoyed. The diggers threw their hats in the air. Danks looked extremely uncomfortable.

Sugden called to Luke: 'Mr Greenwood, you are a lucky man to have such a son. Would that we were all so fortunate.' He rose and went back into Danks' office.

Rebecca embraced her husband. Jack turned towards him. Luke extended his hand for a heartfelt handshake.

'Thank you, Jack,' Luke said simply.

'I just said what was true, father.' He uttered the word uncertainly as if it was in a foreign language. Luke grasped his hand tighter. Jack had made his new start.

A baked joint of lamb stood steaming on the table. There was an abundance of vegetables and, of course, Rebecca's by-now famous bread. The occasion was Marcel and Clee's farewell dinner. Everybody bowed their heads in prayer as Luke led them in grace.

'For what we are about to receive, may the Lord make us truly thankful. And may we be thankful also for all the mercy and deliverance He has shown us this day and in days gone by.' Everybody chorused, 'Amen.' Luke stood to carve the meat as the diners looked with delight on the spread. 'Before we start eating, Rebecca has an important announcement to make.'

Rebecca blushed and dropped her eyes but then rallied and

smiled with inner joy. 'Early in the new year, Luke and I are going to have a baby.'

'Bravo!' shouted Marcel.

'Oh, Mum . . .' Lucy squealed with delight.

Marcel kissed Rebecca on both cheeks. '*Félicitations*, Rebecca.'

Much to Luke's astonishment, Marcel kissed him, too. But the reaction Rebecca and Luke were gladdest about was Jack's. He sat there nodding slightly, a smile as broad and long as a summer's day on his face.

Lin had been invited to share the meal, but had declined, realizing in his wise way that it was a family occasion. He sat in his customary posture, cross-legged in front of the small household shrine. He smoked his huge pipe, and the smoke from this joined with the incense to form huge loops under the canvas roof. He was reading the 'I Ching'. Jack and Clee entered.

'Can we come in, Lin?'

'As always, most welcome. And Clee, most honoured.' He motioned them to sit on the grass mat by his side.

'I've just come to say goodbye, Lin. I'm going back to Melbourne tomorrow.'

'And so pleased you came to say such.'

'Have you read anything more about the future?' Clee asked.

'No. Best if future stay in future. Knowledge of present and past can help, but future . . .' He shook his head.

'You were right about Father. He used to be a lot different from now,' Jack said.

'It is a great gift to be able to change. Very great fortune to change from a boy to a better man. Many people do not get better.'

'Will Jack, do you think?' Clee inquired teasingly.

'Maybe you find out for yourself,' the old Chinaman replied in the same tone. Then he began to smile. His smile grew wider and wider until his slanting eyes disappeared into wreaths of wrinkles. The children looked at each other and began to smile, too.

Marcel had decided to give a final performance before leaving Jericho. They began early because summer had arrived with a rush and they wanted to finish before noon arrived with its smothering heat. Clee, the tomboy, had been replaced by Cleopatre, the artiste. She was dressed in spangled tights and a gaudy silk jerkin, and her cheeks were rouged and her eyes made up.

The diggers and their families pressed closer as Marcel beat on the drum to announce the beginning of the show. 'We would like to offer this performance to you, the people of Jericho, and especially the Greenwood family, for accepting us into your hearts. Soon we will be back and, sparing no expense, we will bring you a bigger and more wonderful show.'

And so the show began. Marcel and Clee did all the favourite tricks: knife-throwing, the stabbing of the swords through the magic chest, the mesmerism; Clee even fired a pistol and Marcel caught the bullet in his teeth. The final act was the one Jack dreaded and yet looked forward to at the same time. Clee was again trussed up with rope, padlocked into a canvas sack, and lowered into a barrel of water. Once again the audience strained forward with bated breath. Jack,

Sean and Lucy frowned. Surely she had been down too long. When they first saw the act, she was just another performer who risked her life, but now she was their friend. The seconds ticked by, the water spilled over the side, then became still. Jack was about to rush forward when Clee erupted from the water, brandishing her ropes.

The audience went wild. But for the Greenwoods, the triumph over death-by-water was a symbol of their own victories, and Jack's the hardest one of all, because he had beaten his past, the strongest enemy of all.

Clee picked up her brush and comb set from an old box which acted as their dressing-table. She placed them in her battered case and snapped it shut.

Jack watched her soulfully, realizing how much he would miss her. 'It's sad . . . isn't it?' he sighed.

'What?'

Jack shrugged. 'Everything's over.'

Clee tightened the straps around her bag and thought about this. Then she turned and smiled at Jack. 'Nothing is ever over. Not really.'

Jack smiled back. He was not sure what she meant, but he would take her word for it.

The sideshow was packed up and stowed on the caravan. Louis was harnessed and waited patiently. Diggers hailed Clee and Marcel Duberau cheerfully and wished them well. Doc had insisted on taking a farewell photograph of them all and was busy setting up his cumbersome contraption. Jack and Lucy mooned around, desolate at losing their friend. Clee was depressed too, but the trouper in her was exhilarated at the prospect of going back on the road. Both girls wore their seed necklaces proudly. Lin had dressed in his best embroidered jacket and pantaloons for the occasion. Sean's usual swagger was a little less cocky – he too would miss Clee.

Suddenly Clee caught sight of Bojinda hanging back behind the stables. She shouted to him. 'Bojinda! Come over.' But Bojinda made no move. Clee ran over and dragged him back. 'Come on. Papa's dying to meet you.' Bojinda arrived before Marcel, who surveyed him admiringly. 'Papa, this is Bojinda. Bojinda, my father.'

They shook hands. 'Bojinda. Bojinda. *Charmant*,' said Marcel.

Bojinda grinned. Jack also had to smile at the French pronunciation of the aborigine name.

Doc had finally got the co-operation of his subjects. 'Settle down, please, ladies and gentlemen. This is art, not a picnic. I say, this is art!'

They all calmed down and tried to keep still. Lucy grabbed Bojinda and hauled him into the group.

'Still as statues now folks. Hold it right there.'

It was a very motley group. Jack smiled bravely in his accustomed way, standing next to his steadfast father. Rebecca, a capable and beautiful woman, stood next to her gentle daughter. The wise old Chinaman rubbed shoulders with the mysterious aborigine. Then there was Marcel, the extravagant showman with his arm around his quicksilver daughter; and the grinning, waggish Sean. Doc, the larger-than-life Mississippi man, shouted out. 'Thank you all. I do believe this will be one of the great compositions of the decade.'

The time of leave-taking could be put off no longer. Clee

stood in front of Jack. 'Goodbye Jack. Come and see our show when we're back this way, won't you.'

Jack stared at her, his heart flipping over in his chest. He was afraid that if he said anything he might burst into tears.

'Well, say goodbye,' Clee urged. But Jack couldn't. They looked long and hard at each other before Clee leaned impetuously forward and gave him a kiss on the cheek. 'You big silly,' said Clee. Jack smiled through his sorrow. Clee gave Lucy a big hug.

In the shade of the verandah across the street, two pairs of eyes watched this display of warmth from the shadows. It was Lovejoy and Jasper.

'Well, Jasper, my friend, I'm not sorry to see the back of them. Thoroughly nasty sorts. Yes, indeed.'

Jasper put his head on one side sympathetically The hurt and loneliness in the miser's words were obvious even to the bird. Lovejoy could hardly bear to watch the scene taking place in front of him which excluded and would always exclude him.

He reached inside his pocket and took out Lucy's musical locket and opened it. The childish lullaby issued forth. He reflected, for an unguarded instant, on the things that might have been had his love of taking not been stronger than his love of giving; but he banished the thought quickly. 'Let's go inside, my friend. This bright sun is giving Uriah a headache.'

He sidled back to where the dark shop was waiting to receive him, and the plunkety-plunk haunting music played more slowly as the spring wound down.

Clee and Marcel had now mounted on to the driving platform of the caravan. There were tears in some eyes as Marcel cracked the whip and Louis moved forward. The last cries of farewell were shouted, Bojinda muttered something in his own tongue, and so did Lin. Everybody waved as the vehicle gathered momentum.

The Greenwoods stood together as a family, amidst the diggings on which they had learnt so much about themselves and each other, waving to the departing illusionists. Jack would not have swapped the happiness he now felt for all the precious ore under his feet, so easily did Luke's hand rest on his shoulder.

X MARKS THE SPOT
Joan de Hamel

'That's the spot. X marks the spot. Find X. Must find X . . .'

Cop the pilot is badly injured when their helicopter crashes on a secret mission, so Peter, Louise and Ross have to try and make their way across the uncharted bush to find the mysterious X. But other people are after it too, and they are unscrupulous dangerous men.

THE RUNAWAY SETTLERS
Elsie Locke

The true story of an Australian family who ran away to New Zealand and became pioneers. They had to go – it was the only thing to do with a father as drunken and brutal as theirs – so Mrs Small and her six children changed their name to Phipps and sailed away secretly. The family's adventures with wild pigs and Maoris, the gold rushes which beckoned the eldest son Bill to try his luck, and Mrs Phipps's daring journey through the Southern Alps with a herd of cattle for sale, make this a story that will long be remembered. It also conjures up a vivid picture of New Zealand in the middle of the nineteenth century.

UNDER THE MOUNTAIN

Maurice Gee

Rachel and Theo Matheson are twins. Apart from both having red hair, there is nothing remarkable about them – or so they think. Imagine their horror, then, when they discover that only they can save the world from dominance by strange, powerful creatures who are waking from a spellbound sleep of thousands of years ...

THE WORLD AROUND THE CORNER

Maurice Gee

When Caroline discovers an old pair of spectacles in her father's junk shop she has no idea how important they are. Even when she puts them on and sees things very differently, she doesn't guess that the safety of another world depends on them. In a race against time she has to tackle the ghastly Grimbles and keep her promise to return the spectacles to their rightful owners.

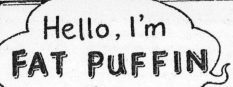